ARCANE RISING

THE DARKLAND DRUIDS - BOOK ONE

NICOLE R. TAYLOR

Arcane Rising (The Darkland Druids - Book One) by
Nicole R. Taylor

Copyright © 2020 by Nicole R. Taylor

All rights reserved.

This book is written in British/AU English.

No part of this book may be reproduced in any form or by any electronic or mechanical means, including information storage and retrieval systems, without written permission from the author, except for the use of brief quotations in a book review.

www.nicolertaylorwrites.com

Cover Design: Pixie Covers & Nicole R. Taylor

Edited by: Silvia Curry

1

Gordan Quarrie had been fighting out of control bushfires for close to two months when they finally came.

He was riding on the back of the backup tanker from Lidcombe—a suburb west of Sydney—when he saw *it* lingering amongst the charred eucalyptus forest.

Leaning out the window, he looked back at the shadow. It'd been years since he'd caught the scent of them and this time, they were closer than ever.

Thumping his fist on the side of the truck, he called, "Can you pull over here?"

"Here?" The driver eased up on the accelerator and pulled off the road, the truck's wheels bumping over the uneven ground beside the bitumen. He turned in his seat and peered at Gordan, his protective helmet askew on his head.

"The front is still a click away," the man beside him said.

"I want to check the containment lines," he told the crew.

"On your own?" the driver asked. "We're not supposed to go solo."

"I know, but there's another unit up there." He tapped the walkie in his coat pocket. "I'll radio."

He leapt out of the tanker and sent them on their way. Checking for traffic in both directions on the highway, he legged it across and into the already burned fire field.

No matter how many seasons he served, Gordan was always startled by the lack of traffic where there would usually be a stream of holiday makers heading to the Blue Mountains.

Today, the road had been closed on either side of the range and nothing was getting through, save for those fleeing the fire front and the firefighters rushing towards it.

He adjusted his coat, cursing as his slick fingers rubbed against the inside seam of his gloves. The gear they had to wear was thick and cumbersome, and he sweated like a pig, but it protected his skin from the radiant heat—which was much more of a risk than open flame or stray embers.

In the distance, about half a kilometre away, he could see the telltale flash of yellow and red—the back-burning crew checking their containment line.

But between him and them, he saw the shadow waiting.

Their luck had finally run out. It'd been quiet few

decades, but deep down, he knew it was only a matter of time before someone came looking. She was too important for them not to. In a world where creatures of power were desperate for domination, they'd never be safe. At least, not for long.

The creature flashed through the charred trees, leaving glowing footprints in its wake. Embers flared and he cursed. It was an elemental solider, its power unhindered now that the Witches had allowed the way to their twisted realm remain open.

Human in shape, its soul was nothing but fury. A shadow of the world it had once come from, the solider was a pawn in an ancient war for dominance that would likely rage for all of time. A war that would continue to claim innocent lives, no matter the consequences. It was a tale as old as the hills—the never-ending cycle of violence. The lust for power through dominance was a corruption he could never stomach.

Gordan knew it was an idiot move coming out here to face it, but if he hadn't, it would have followed him to the front where he wouldn't have been able to stop it from killing him and the others on the Lidcombe crew. Then, with him out of the way, nothing would stop it from finding Elspeth.

He wouldn't let it happen. *He couldn't.*

"Your time has come," the solider said, the words dripping from its blackened mouth. "Where is the girl?"

"Go back to your master and tell them she doesn't belong to anyone," he snarled. "She is not theirs."

Its black eyes began to glow—crimson at first, then bright orange as the temperature rose around them.

Flame flickered, emerging from underneath the already charred surface layer of the burned undergrowth, and the creature drew the embers into the air. They began to swirl, gathering more sparks, and a front erupted with a loud *woosh*.

Gordan held up his arm to shield his face, calling on his Colours to deflect the radiating heat.

"You can't have her!" he shouted over the roaring flame. "You hear me? *You can't have her!*"

The creature stalked towards him, pitch-black and menacing, unafraid of Gordan's power. "She needs to be with her people, *fealltóir*," it rasped, speaking in a stranger's voice. "You can't hide her forever."

"*You can't have her,*" he snarled again. "You can send all the soldiers you want, but I will be there to stop every one of them. Every failed attempt will leave you empty-handed and another of your evil kind sent into the void."

The creature stood before him, twisting with flame. "Is that so?"

The screech of sirens broke through their tense stand-off and they both looked into the smoke at the same time, both with different intents.

Through the haze, Gordan could see a crew of firefighters race towards him, hoses in hand with the truck creeping behind. They were trying to save him, dumping a torrent of water on the approaching flames, but they couldn't see the enemy hiding within the firestorm.

Blue and red lights flashed through the haze as he shouted for them to stay back, but his cries went unheard. His radio chirped—the desperate calls distorted by static.

The fire roared behind him, spurred on by the elemental force twisting in the tornado. They'd all be killed if he couldn't stop the solider. It had to die here and now before it could get to Elspeth.

"I'm sorry, sweetheart," he murmured as if she could hear him. He took off his helmet and tossed it to the ground. "There's so much you don't know, but I have to keep you safe. This is the only way. *I'm sorry*."

The creature lunged and he leapt into its searing embrace, pouring his Colour into the twisted monster. It screeched in agony as Gordan's essence drove into its core, shattering the soul that helped its impure body cling to life.

Fire raged around them, engulfing their bodies.

He knew he was only buying her time. Destiny would lead her home. He just hoped he'd taught her enough that she would understand how to find her way.

With his last breath, he sent his love to his daughter…and a prayer for her future.

I'll never forget the sound of that knock on the door.

A man and a woman stood on the porch, both wearing navy-blue police uniforms—their vests laden with radios and cameras, and light-blue shirts underneath their bulletproof vests.

"Elspeth Quarrie?" the woman asked, taking off her cap.

I nodded, the scent of burning eucalyptus thick in the air. The air quality had been terrible for the last month, the smoke haze from the fires covering Sydney from top to bottom.

"I'm Sergeant Peters and this is Constable Guthrie. May we come inside?"

Yeah…I'd never forget that day. What I was doing. Who I was waiting for. What I'd been dreaming. The Christmas Day I'd just spent with my dad. Just the two of us.

I'd just graduated university and my whole life was ahead of me. The television was turned onto the news, my mobile phone was open on the government emergency app, and the air conditioning was running at a breezy twenty-two degrees Celsius. I should have been working on my resume, but my mind was elsewhere.

I'd never dealt well with the heat. Neither had my dad, but we lived in one of the hottest and driest climates in our changing world—Australia—and with it came certain dangers. Venomous snakes and spiders were one thing, but the constant threat of drought and fire was a reality no one could escape. Not even the big cities could ignore the looming smoke on the horizon anymore.

Bushfires had been raging across most of the country for months, and my dad was out there, fighting the impossible inferno with the thousands of other career and volunteer firefighters.

As an environmental scientist, Dad's skills were in high demand during the emergency. He could predict shifts in air currents and weather patterns that were useful on the ground. He could look at the growth in a forest and the curve of the land to know where to best put in containment lines. He coordinated back burning that saved towns from being completely wiped off the map. Knowing where the fire would leap or where the embers would blow was crucial in saving homes and lives.

After the first month, he came home looking like he'd aged a decade. Soot was permanently caked under his fingernails and his eyes were… Well, he looked haunted by the things he'd seen.

Two days later, on Boxing Day, he was packing up his uniform to hit the ground again. He was the only person I had in the entire world. Why did he have to go?

I have the power to help, he told me. *And when the Earth and her creatures cry out in pain, we should answer with our whole hearts.*

So when the knock came on the front door, I already knew who stood on the other side.

The visitors the family of firefighters dreaded most during the summer.

It was the sound of your entire life being torn out from under your feet.

That night, I lay in bed and stared at the ceiling. Things went that way for a couple of weeks, even as flowers began to show up at the house, along with letters from the government and casseroles from the neighbours.

We'd kept to ourselves, but it seemed Dad had been loved by many—no matter how secretive he thought he'd been.

Dad never spoke about my mother or his home in Scotland. He never talked about his family or what his life had been like before we came to Australia. I never knew what happened to my mum or why we'd come here. It was as if our lives had begun the moment he carried me off the plane.

I'd shared everything with him. Not just the adventurous Scottish spirit that ran through our blood, but the things I dreamed about and the future I saw for myself. It was him and I against the world, but I was all grown up now and with age came the unfortunate responsibility of knowledge.

I searched through his things, looking for a birth certificate, a photograph, or a scrap of paper that would tell me where he'd come from or who my mother was. I found nothing—not even a secret diary or a hidden compartment. For all his accolades and achievements, my father was a ghost.

I was a ghost.

I stopped looking for work. I stopped caring. I didn't know how to go on without him.

So, I walked. At first, I took the train into Sydney and wandered around the markets and the harbour.

I watched people go about their business, wondering where they were going in such a rush. Did they have someone to go home to? Friends? Family? Kids? None of those things had ever been in my life…at least, not for very long.

I was a terrible friend, always enjoying my own company over that of others. Any friendships I did have fizzled out pretty quickly, and it was the same with boyfriends. Either they were only interested in one thing or I couldn't connect with them. Life was a mould, but I couldn't bend far enough to fit inside the white picket fence.

As I walked the city streets, I had a sudden sense that I never really belonged here. Australia had been my home, but I wasn't a part of it. My dad had been my anchor to this place. Now that he was gone, I was adrift.

There had to be something else…this couldn't be it.

That's when I saw it.

Standing outside the travel agency, Flight Centre, I stared at the poster in the window, my eyes drinking in the rolling hills of the Scottish Highlands like they were an oasis in the middle of a charred forest.

The world fell away, and I imagined myself walking through the wild landscape, the cool wind on my cheeks, the drizzling rain misting through the greyish sky, and the trickling of a creek feeding into a vast loch. The absence of people and the pull of the Earth.

The blood in my veins hummed and I pressed my palm against the window. An unfamiliar longing was rising, charging my body with an almost electric excitement.

The sound of a car horn blaring broke me out of my daze and I blinked, snatching my hand away from the window. I rubbed my palms up and down my arms, chilled as if the heat of the summer day hadn't reached me at all.

I glanced at the people walking past, my cheeks heating with embarrassment, but they didn't seem to notice me at all.

A daydream, I thought. *Just a daydream.*

I glanced at the poster of the Scottish Highlands again and my heart skipped a beat. Hardly understanding what I was doing, I opened the door to speak with the travel agent.

2

The first thing I noticed about Scotland was the cold. Then how green and lush everything was compared to the dry, dead brown of the drought-ravaged Australian countryside.

I stood outside the large grey building on the Royal Mile, in Edinburgh's Old Town, looking up at the stone façade. The sign above the door read, *Campbell's Serviced Apartments*. At least I was in the right spot.

Rolling my suitcase behind me, and following the directions on my printed booking confirmation, I went into the foyer. The lines were all wobbly, the last of the ink made the picture of the building look like an old-fashioned sepia portrait. That's what I got for making last-minute travel arrangements based on a hallucination.

The instructions said to knock on the door of the ground-floor apartment, so that's what I did.

The door opened, revealing a robust older lady. Her short grey hair was a wild mop and her brown, cable-knit jumper looked handmade, but her eyes were warm and friendly.

"Mrs. Campbell?" I asked. "I'm Elspeth Quarrie. I—"

"Ah, there you are," she declared, her accent almost musical to my ears. "You're a pretty lass. Let me look at you."

"Uh…okay?"

She'd obviously set the bar low, considering I wasn't anything special to look at. My hair was mousey blonde with touches of auburn—the flecks of red brought out the green in my eyes. I was on the taller side, but neither overweight nor slim. I was simply a normal woman. Average, unremarkable, but passable if looks was what it came down to.

"I thought the fairies had taken you," she went on, completing her assessment without comment. "I was expecting you hours ago."

"Uh, no fairies, just a long line at customs."

"The fools," Mrs. Campbell scoffed and gestured for me to follow her up the stairs. "I gather their computers were broken again or some such. They usually are. There'll be a scathing write up about it in the newspaper tomorrow."

"Yes, they were." I gathered she wasn't a fan of technology. "Everyone had to wait to get an old-fashioned stamp."

The stairs creaked as we began to climb.

"There are three other apartments in the house," Mrs. Campbell said, leading me up the narrow flight. "You're here for a month, but if you want to stay longer, let me know as soon as you can. It's winter and past Hogmanay, but people still want to stay on the Mile. You seem like a sweet lass, and a sight quieter than the regular louts that rent the place, so I'd rather give it to you. But as I said, you'll have to let me know."

"Oh no, I won't be any trouble, Mrs. Campbell," I told her, dragging my suitcase up the stairs behind me.

"So, what are you? Writer? Artist? Please don't tell me you're one of those *digital nomads*."

"What do you have against digital nomads?"

Mrs. Campbell turned and gave me the evil eye. "They're the worst, lass. They pretend to 'work' on their computers, eat up all the WiFi with their *streaming*, and come in at all hours pissed up past the eyeballs! And all of it captured with a camera on a long stick pointing at their own faces."

I bit my bottom lip to stop myself from laughing and shrugged. "I'm just looking to find some information about my family and maybe a little sightseeing."

"Oh!" she declared. "You're a historian, then? How lovely!"

"Sure." I didn't know what I was, but I didn't want to burst her bubble. I'd graduated with one of those useless Arts degrees in the hopes of one day doing something creative like work in an art gallery or a museum, but that day seemed like it belonged in another life.

We reached the landing and I leaned against the wall, catching my breath. This city was making me feel severely inadequate in the fitness department and I'd only been here an hour.

"Here we are." Mrs. Campbell unlocked the door and handed me the key. "Now, everything you need is inside, but if you have any questions, *read the book.*"

I gathered that was my cue that she was releasing me into the wild, so I thanked her and pushed open the door, my suitcase wheels bumping over the threshold.

The apartment was a one-bedroom with a little bathroom. A living area made up the rest of the space with a kitchenette, couch, TV, and a two-seater dining table by the window.

Outside, I could see the Royal Mile and the little bus stop below. The building was situated at the bottom end, away from most of the noise, but it was busy enough for the middle of the afternoon.

A book and a box of shortbread biscuits—obviously bought from one of the many souvenir shops downstairs—sat on the dining table. I left my suitcase by the bed and slid into a chair and sighed. I was going to get strong thighs walking up all those stairs…and the hills! Edinburgh had so many inclines to traverse it was almost a punishment, or a cruel joke at tourists' expense.

I picked up the book—which turned out to be a plastic display folder—and flipped through the pages. Liking my new surroundings already, I smiled at the thought the landlady had put into the information. There was even a bus timetable slipped into one of the pockets.

Mrs. Campbell seemed like a nice old lady, but I got the feeling I shouldn't cross her, otherwise her inner dragon would appear.

I looked out the window again as jet lag tried to pull me towards the bedroom. Shaking my head, I rubbed my scratchy eyes and grabbed my bag. I'd just spent thirty hours either on an aeroplane or queuing up to get on one, and now that I was finally here, I wanted to explore.

Secretly, I wanted to find my father.

I hesitated at the door, my hand pausing on the handle, and I sniffed my armpit. Cringing, I dumped my bag back onto the table. *First things first, Elspeth. A shower to wash your stink off, then exploring.*

It was only polite, after all.

Greyfriars Kirk was nestled at one end of Edinburgh's Old Town, and while it didn't look far on the map, my lungs were burning by the time I found the gates.

Thick grass covered the lawns and there was a gravesite, headstone, or plaque everywhere I looked. They were even set into the walls of the cottages backing onto the kirkyard. At the centre was the church itself, complete with modern upgrades. They still held services and a light shone from within. It calmed me a little knowing someone else was about and I wasn't the only fool wandering in a graveyard full of ghosts at twilight.

Many of the headstones were large and ornate, with statues of angels and crosses. Some were buried underground, and others—who were obviously rich and important—had mausoleums with locked doors.

I stopped at the end of the row and looked up at the carvings on the last gravesite. I studied the skull and crossbones—*and* the dancing skeleton— wondering why anyone would want to put such a thing on their tombstone. They were a morbid lot in the sixteenth century—I wondered why. Underneath, the words *memento mori* were carved into the stone. *Memento Mori*, remember you must die.

I thought of my dad, and the news the police had brought with them on New Year's Eve. There wasn't anything left to bury. He was swallowed up by the fire in the blink of an eye. There was nothing the crew could do to save him. *We're sorry for your loss.*

There would be no grave. No place to go and mourn. Nothing but memory.

I shivered and buried my hands into my coat pockets, realising a mist had begun to form in the lengthening shadows.

Turning away, I walked along the path, my boots crunching against the damp gravel. A plaque on the stone wall told me all about the city's original outer defences—the Flodden Wall.

After the Scottish forces were defeated by the English at the battle of Flodden in 1513—and resulting in the death of their king, James IV— Edinburgh's officials were frightened that the victorious army would besiege the city. The wall was built to defend their territory.

I pressed my palm against the stone and imagined the army on the field and the people in the city—who must have been terrified of what would become of them without a monarch on the throne. Maybe they didn't care. Food and shelter must have been more pressing matters for the common folk of the time, rather than who governed them.

I walked under the arch, finding another stretch of gravesites beyond. The mist seemed to thicken, and I glanced over my shoulder. It was spooky without anyone else around and I began to wonder if the kirkyard was closed. I checked my watch, finding it was almost four, but being winter, it was already dark.

Streetlights were turning on, bathing the kirkyard in orange light and the sudden change was eerie. *Must be the dancing skeletons and ghost stories creeping me out.*

The row of gravestones shimmered and began to lengthen, multiplying into the distance. The city faded and disappeared, leaving me standing in an unknown world.

I stumbled and my heart began to race. *What in the world…?*

Frightened, I turned and almost smacked into a man standing behind me. I yelped as his smile widened, his pointed teeth glimmering in the orange glow of the lamplight.

I was frozen to the spot, staring at him in shock. His eyes were black; there were no whites or iris'—just two pools of pitch-black nothingness.

He grabbed me, moving like a bolt of lightning, and his hands bit into the flesh of my arms. I screamed as my knees buckled, terror gripping my senses as blinding pain tore through my head.

A shadowy shape leapt out from behind a headstone, barking and baring its teeth. The dog latched onto the man's leg, growling and shaking its jaws back and forth.

The force of the dog's attack dislodged the man's grip on me, and I staggered back a few steps, my breath catching as I held my throbbing head.

A second man loomed behind them—dark and tall amongst the tendrils of the mist—and his gaze fell onto mine. He almost looked startled to see me there, but it was only for a moment before his expression turned thunderous. He moved towards me faster than my eyes could follow, but it was enough to snap me back into reality. The reality where I was being attacked by monsters in a misty graveyard.

I fled through the kirkyard, passing underneath the arch, desperately searching for the church where I'd seen the light on inside. Mist swirled around my ankles as I ran, but all I found were more tombs.

Stone skeletons and menacing angels stood silent in the gloom, fuelling the terror in my heart. Skidding to a stop, I turned around, searching for a way out of my nightmare.

The mist had swallowed the city and the sounds of the men…and the dog. It'd been a huge thing, like a German Shepard, only all black. No wonder I hadn't seen it.

But that man… His teeth… *His eyes.*

Spotting the gate through the mist, I took off again, crossing the grass. It was muddy and I almost slipped on my arse, but I made it without falling. My fear began to ease as the city appeared.

A car whooshed by on the narrow road, reminding me that I wasn't alone. No one else was around, but there had to be people in the houses. I fumbled in my bag, wondering what the emergency number for the police was in Scotland.

"Where are you going?"

The sound of a male voice caused me to spin and I came face to face with the second man—the one with the dog.

Before I could react, he'd grabbed my arm and nearly pulled me off my feet.

"Let me go!" I cried as he began to drag me towards a narrow lane.

First him and his dog were saving me from whatever that other guy was, and now he was trying to kidnap me? I didn't have a clue what was going on. It was a jet-lag-induced psychosis brought about by my repressed grief over my dad's death. It wasn't right not to cry when your only parent died. This was my punishment, right?

"Don't fash yourself," the man said. "I'm only trying to help."

"By dragging me into the alley so you can—" I choked on my words and began to panic. I didn't come all this way only to be kidnapped, assaulted, and murdered. There was no way in hell I was going to become another number.

"Who are you?" he asked. "Where did you come from?"

"Your worst nightmares, creep!" I shouted.

With a cry of rage, I swung my fist at the man's face, startling him enough so I could stamp my boot on his foot. He yelped in surprise and his grip on my arm loosened. I wrenched myself free and took off, sprinting down the road with energy I never knew I had.

And I didn't look back.

3

———

I didn't know how long I'd been running before I saw a police station up ahead.

Why was it so hard to find a cop shop in this city? *Budget cuts*, I thought. *It's always budget cuts.*

I hurtled through the front door and slapped my palms down onto the counter, startling the young man at the desk. He spilled his coffee, the brown liquid dripping onto his trousers.

"*Christ Almighty,*" he exclaimed in a thick accent. "Will ye watch the door, lass!"

"I'd like to report a crime," I declared between heaving breaths. "Someone just tried to kidnap me."

"Attempted kidnapping, ye say?" He looked at me with a raised eyebrow. "Please take a seat."

My mouth dropped open. "Take a seat?"

"Yes," he said, brushing at the coffee stain on his trousers. "Take. A. *Seat.*"

Behind the partition, a man rolled a chair across

the room and leaned back so he could see me. He seemed to be in his early thirties, lean and muscular, and dressed in a navy suit with an off-white shirt and loosened black tie. He smoothed his palm through his close-cropped hair and smiled at me.

"Don't fash yourself, lass," he said. "I'll hear your report."

The officer at the window looked taken aback. "But—"

"I said, I'll listen to the lass' report, *constable*," he snapped. "Now bugger off and get yourself a stale doughnut to go with that shite you call coffee."

The constable scowled and scurried away from the desk, cursing under his breath as he disappeared through the mostly empty offices.

"I apologise for my colleague's briskness," the man said, standing and moving towards the counter. "There's a reason some people are assigned desk jobs."

I'll say.

"Detective Murray," he added, holding out his hand. "And you are?"

"Elspeth Quarrie," I replied, shaking his hand. "I, uh…" His grasp was firm and confident—everything I wasn't—and I flushed.

"You look like you've had quite the fright, lass. Can I get you something warm to drink?"

"No, I…" I sighed and nodded. "Yeah. That would be great."

"Tea? Coffee?"

"Tea."

The detective smiled and rounded the front counter. "Let's go into one of the interview rooms, hey? It's warmer and a little more private."

He ushered me down the hall into a back room. Inside, it looked just like interview rooms did on TV. There was a stainless-steel table bolted to the floor with two chairs on either side and a mirror covered one end of the room, which was likely two-way mirror. A surveillance camera was also built into one of the corners, where it was out of reach by the unfortunate interviewee.

There was nothing else in here for obvious reasons.

"Have a seat and I'll be back in a moment," Detective Murray said. "The chairs are quite cold, I'm afraid."

"Oh…" I blinked, and he flashed a smile before he left to fetch my tea.

I sat on the chair, frowning when I found it to be ice cold. The chill spread through my arse cheeks and I snorted. A brilliant end to a brilliant day of disasters. First the airport was on the fritz, then…

Oh hell, what was I doing here?

How was I meant to tell the police I'd been grabbed in a dark, misty graveyard by a man with pointy teeth and black eyes? And that was only the half of it. They'd think I was crazy, send me to a hospital for a psychological evaluation, and I'd be deported back to Australia.

I looked at the mirror and studied the reflection of the interview room, avoiding myself. The hairs on the back of my neck stood up and I shivered. Shoving my hands into my coat pockets, I began to wonder if coming to Scotland was a mistake. After all, Dad had left for a reason.

When Detective Murray returned, he held a disposable cup in one hand and a notepad and pen in the other. Suddenly, I felt extremely foolish.

"The longer I sit here, the sillier this all seems," I told him. "I don't want to waste your time."

I went to stand but he shook his head. "Don't worry about that," he said, setting the cup down in front of me. "If it puts your mind at ease, then I'll listen. It's my job."

I sighed. Well, if it was his *job*.

He sat on opposite side of the table and clicked the button on the pen in his hand. "Are you a tourist or do you live in Edinburgh?"

I blinked, the night's events and my exhausted state started to catch up with me.

"Your accent," he prodded.

"I, uh… I'm a tourist, I suppose. I have a UK passport, but I live in Australia. My dad was Scottish."

"Was?"

I hesitated. "He died recently."

"Oh, I see." He frowned and leaned back in his chair. "I'm sorry for your loss."

I looked down at the paper cup, watching a stray tea leaf float in the milky drink. He didn't press for more information and I was thankful. I didn't want to talk about my dad's death. *Ever.*

"How long have you been in the UK?"

"I got here this afternoon."

The detective paused for a moment then said, "Only a few hours? What a welcome. I personally apologise on behalf of the Scottish people."

I managed a tiny smile and looked up at him. His eyes sparkled and an eerie calmness flowed through me.

"What happened tonight, Miss Quarrie?" he asked, his tone gentle. "Take your time. We're in no rush."

I reached for the tea, but my hands began to shake so I pulled back and glanced at the two-way mirror. The image was distorted—a fault in the glass most likely—and the detective's reflection wavered as he leaned forwards.

"We're alone," he said, following my gaze. "No one's watching. Everything you tell me is confidential, for the report."

"Well, I... I was excited to see the city, even though I was tired," I began. "*Am* tired, I mean. I heard it's better to stay awake until your regular bedtime in a new time zone to stop jet lag. So, I went to Greyfriars Kirk. I heard it was beautiful there, and it didn't seem far on the map... But the light faded faster than I realised, and it was hilly..."

"It gets dark quite early here during the winter,"

Detective Murray explained. "Most visitors don't realise."

"It's the country's location in correlation with the North Pole," I said. "The closer to a pole, the shorter days become in wintertime. They're longer in the summer."

The detective chuckled. "That's right. Are you a scientist?"

"Uh, my dad was. He taught me a lot of things growing up."

"I see." He gestured for me to continue with my report.

"There weren't any other people around, but lights were on in the church, so I thought nothing of it." I went on to tell him how the man came out of the shadows and grabbed me, carefully omitting the part about the eyes and teeth. Then I added everything that came next with the second man and the dog.

Detective Murray was thoughtful for a moment. "Did it seem to you that they knew one another?"

"I don't think so…"

"And the dog. A *black* German Shepard?"

"This all sounds so silly," I said lamely. "I don't know why I—" I swallowed hard, fighting back tears.

"It's not," Detective Murray said. "If a woman is threatened by two men on the street, we want to know about it. Don't be afraid of sounding silly. The police take these matters extremely seriously, Miss Quarrie.

We want more women to speak up about violence against them. It's how progress is made."

I began to worry the hem of my jumper. "Well, uh, when you put it that way…"

"I'll have the constable file your report and the descriptions of the two men. We'll do what we can to track them down."

"Are you sure you want to give it to him?" I wondered out loud.

"Aye, an astute remark." Detective Murray laughed. "Serves him right for speaking to you the way he did." He looked at his watch and clicked his pen. "It's the end of my shift. How about I give you a ride back to your hotel? It wouldn't be very policeman-like of me to send you out there on your own in the dark. Not after the night you've had."

"Oh, I can get a taxi. It's fine."

"It's no bother, Miss Quarrie," he told me. "It would be my pleasure to end your first day in Scotland on a brighter note."

I paused a moment. It wasn't likely he was going to be the third predator I'd meet today. Besides, he was a cop.

There are crooked cops, Elspeth, I thought. *Oh, shut up.*

"That would be great, if it's not too much trouble," I said. "I don't really know the way back."

He grinned and gestured to the door. "Not a problem at all, lass. It would be my pleasure."

Detective Murray was true to his word and saw me to the front door of Mrs. Campbell's serviced apartments on the Royal Mile.

When he pulled his unmarked police car into the end of the bus stop, I was surprised when he got out the car with me. Parking illegally *and* a little presumptuous… I'd have to remember that.

"Well, here we are, Miss Quarrie," he said, looking up at the building. "Safe and sound."

"Elspeth," I said. "Miss Quarrie makes me sound like a schoolteacher."

"Elspeth then." The detective chuckled, his breath vaporising in the chilled air. "Then it's only fair you stop calling me detective and call me Owen."

I nodded a little awkwardly.

"Well, we'll keep an eye out for the perpetrators," he told me. "If we find anything, I'll let you know, and if there's anything you need…"

It took me a moment to realise he was offering services above and beyond what normal cops provided. I felt my cheeks heat and I didn't know where to look. He *was* handsome, but my lack of romantic experience was totally showing all over my face. I mean, it wasn't like I was a virgin or anything; I just didn't know why anyone would be interested in a mousy woman like me. *Oh, shut up, Elspeth.*

"Oh, uh…" I swallowed hard. "Thank you."

"Well, here's my number." He handed me a white business card emblazoned with the Scottish police logo. "If you need anything, please call. It's no trouble."

Owen flashed me another smile and strode back to his car. I watched as he drove away, the business card still clutched in-between my fingers like it was going to self-destruct in T-minus ten seconds.

A dot of rain hit my nose and I rubbed it away. Sighing, I pocketed the card and went inside. At least my nerves about the strange happenings in the kirkyard were calmed, but they'd been replaced with a whole other set of unknowns. Either that, or I was overthinking things.

The moment I stepped into the building, Mrs. Campbell's door opened and she came charging out.

"Was that a policeman I saw you with?" She pulled aside the curtain on the foyer door and peered out at the street. "A handsome one, too. Are you all right, lass?"

"That was Detective Owen Murray," I told her, realising just how much of a busybody my temporary landlady really was. "I ran into a little trouble and he offered me a ride back."

"Must have been a wee bit more than a little trouble to get seen home by a *detective*." She clucked her tongue and began to check my extremities. It was a little too personal for a woman I'd just met, and I extracted myself as politely as I could manage.

"It was nothing, really," I muttered. "Just walking where I shouldn't, I guess."

"Don't downplay yourself, lass," Mrs. Campbell

said with a frown. "Times may be changing, but they're still tough for women, no doubt."

I wasn't going to be able to escape without telling her what had happened, so I told her about the men who attacked me in Greyfriars Kirkyard. Her expression changed throughout my tale, morphing from concerned, to interested, to surprised, and thoughtful in the span of three minutes.

"My, my," she said, wringing her wrinkly hands. "What a welcome Edinburgh has given you, lass. A man and a dog you say?"

"And another weird-looking guy…" I shivered, recalling his pointed teeth and black eyes.

Mrs. Campbell pressed her hands on my cheeks and frowned. "Would you like me to make you something to eat? You look pale."

For a lady I'd only met a few hours ago and was renting a holiday apartment from, she was acting rather grandmotherly right now. Somehow, I doubted she was like this with all her tenants.

"I'm okay, Mrs. Campbell. I haven't had a good night's sleep in a few days. It's a long way from Sydney, and no one can ever sleep in economy."

"Well, you'll be safe here. I'll see to it."

"Thank you." I seemed to be saying that a lot lately.

Mrs. Campbell returned to peeking out the curtains as I made a hasty exit up the crooked stairs. Closing my apartment door behind me, I flicked on the light and heaved a sigh of relief. I'd led a pretty mundane life for twenty-five years, and I'd made up for it all in one day.

Shuffling across the room, I practically fell into bed, only lingering long enough to change out of my clothes.

The moment my head hit the pillow, sleep took over and the night's adventures melted away—but I knew the memories would be waiting for me in the morning.

4

What are you doing here? Get out! Run before it's too late!

I woke with a start, the last of my dream fading into nothingness.

Get out? I rubbed my eyes and looked around the little bedroom, gathering my wits. Exhausted dreams rarely made sense, but it still took me a moment to remember where I was.

I must have slept for at least ten hours because my limbs were stiff and ached as I rolled over. Through the door I could see the window by the dining table where beyond was a grey sky and the sharp edges of the building next door. A moss-green drainpipe crawled up the side of the dark stone, looking like a thick vine, and disappeared out of view.

The longer I lay there and stared at the day, the more last night's chaos seemed like something that had happened to someone else.

I blinked and a vision of the man with pointed teeth and black eyes appeared like a smack in the face. Sitting up, I rubbed my eyes and kicked my legs out of bed.

It didn't make sense. Was it some kind of extreme body modification? Eyeball tattoos? Contact lenses? And why did I think of eyeball tattoos *before* contact lenses?

What would he have done with me if he'd managed to drag me off? It was a question that didn't bear answering.

Who are you? Where did you come from? The other man's questions rang through my mind and I shivered. *I'd like to know the answer to that too, buddy.*

There must be somewhere I could search some historical archives—or births, deaths, and marriages. Maybe Mrs. Campbell would know.

Determined not to let the city crush my spirits, I decided to go out and resume my mission somewhere a little more populated. I showered and dressed, stuffing some of the shortbread biscuits Mrs. Campbell had left into my mouth.

I was still spitting crumbs when I went downstairs.

A man was tinkering with the door, screwing something into the jamb with a power drill. A toolbox was at his feet, and he wore a sweatshirt that read *Edinburgh Security Systems PTY LTD*.

Mrs. Campbell was pacing behind him like a restless fox, supervising his work with a keen eye.

When she heard me on the creaky stairs, she threw her hands into the air and grinned up at me.

"Elspeth, there you are, lass," she declared. "I thought it was past time to get some extra security installed." She handed me a little grey plastic tag. "Pop this on your keys. The man tells me it's called a *fob*."

"Uh, thank you." I wiped the biscuit crumbs from my mouth and took the tag, slipping it into my pocket.

This place was getting stranger as time went on… and not much time had passed. I wondered what chaos today would bring. Fingers crossed it was a little less menacing than last night's adventure.

"Where are you off to today?" Mrs. Campbell asked, slyly ogling the installer's rear end.

"I thought I might walk up to the castle," I said, wondering if I should frown or laugh at her antics.

"Oh, good. Lots of people up there on the Mile. The castle is expensive, but everyone should go inside at least once." She turned back to the workman and resumed her staring.

"Mrs. Campbell?" She looked at me and tilted her head to the side. "Do you know where I might be able to find some public information about births and deaths? And other things like marriages and census records? I'm researching my family tree and—"

"You can always look on the internet for that kind of thing. I'm a great fan of that Ancestor website, but you can go to the National Records office on Princes Street. It costs money, last I heard."

"Thank you. I may as well walk over there and have a look before going to the castle."

I gave her a small wave and stepped around the workman and out onto the street. The air was crisp, and I was glad I had the foresight to pack my coat. It was a thin leather jacket, but it kept most of the chill out.

"She's such polite lass," I heard Mrs. Campbell say to the workman. Then she bellowed after me, "Don't forget it gets dark at half three!"

<hr>

The National Records of Scotland sat directly at one end of North Bridge in the New Town of Edinburgh.

After five minutes in the place, I was told there was no room available for record searches and I'd have to make a booking online to reserve a desk. The fee was fifteen pounds a day, which was at least thirty Australian dollars—not cheap by any means.

I thanked the clerk and went outside, feeling a little deflated over the whole thing. I should have done more research, but my trip was so last minute that I'd done nothing but book a flight and the accommodation to go with it.

Outside was a statue of the Duke of Wellington on a rearing horse, the original brass long turned green due to the weather. I looked up at it and wondered what he would do. Wellington was a general, right? No, he was a prime minister.

I blinked up at the statue. We were definitely in two different leagues.

"Elspeth!"

My heart leapt at the sound of someone shouting my name. I turned to find Owen walking towards me, his imposing stature caused people to dart out of his way.

"Twice in as many days," he declared, flashing a five-million-megawatt smile at me. "How are you this morning?"

My heart fluttered. "Much better."

"I'm glad to see you out and not too shaken by your ordeal last night."

I didn't want to talk about it, so I veered the conversation elsewhere. "What are you doing today? I thought you'd be out working."

"Oh, it's my rostered afternoon off today," he explained. "I was doing a few things in town when I spotted you."

My nerves tingled at the vagueness of his explanation. *Don't be so critical, Elspeth. It's just the lingering shock after what had happened last night.*

That was one of my faults, I supposed. Overthinking, critical, suspicious—all excuses for not putting myself out there more.

"Don't worry about your report," he added. "I spent the morning canvassing Greyfriars with some constables."

"Did you find anything?"

"Nothing, unfortunately. The kirk's CCTV wasn't

working and it was dark. A lot of tourists visit to see the graves and the grass is all churned up, so there wasn't much to find." He smiled in an attempt to reassure me. "Your descriptions of the two men have been circulated, so all of Edinburgh's officers will be on the lookout."

I guess it was as much as I could hope for. Knowing those men were still out there was a little unnerving, but I wasn't going to let it stop me from enjoying my holiday.

"This is nice," he said, plucking the scarf around my neck.

I looked down at my first Scottish purchase. The scarf was green, blue, and black tartan, supposedly made from lambswool, though it felt acrylic to me.

"Oh, I didn't think to bring one so I got it this morning from one of those tacky souvenir shops," I explained. "It's summer back home."

"It's called a Black Watch tartan," Owen told me. "It's for those who have no family tartan of their own."

I snorted at the irony and shook my head. It was the only colour I liked out of the thirty variations on display. *Another omen.*

"What did I say?" Owen frowned and looked up at the archives.

"Nothing… It's just I didn't come here to be a tourist. I wanted to learn more about my family."

"Your father?"

I nodded, remembering that I'd mentioned it last

night. "He never really spoke about where he came from, only that he immigrated from Scotland when I was a baby. He passed away before I could ask the hard questions."

"Oh, I see," he said thoughtfully. "Was the archive no help?"

"I had to book a seat to do a day search, or whatever they called it, but all the spots were taken."

"So you really don't know anything?" He raised his eyebrows. "Grandparents? Aunts? Uncles?"

I shook my head. "Nothing."

If he thought it was strange, he didn't let it show on his face. "So, you want to find out more about your family tree?"

"Yeah, I'm trying to." It was beginning to feel like something was stopping me. Dad never talked about his past, and now it seemed Scotland itself was trying its hardest to join the party. "I was hoping to find out something—anything—but it seems like Scotland has a grudge against me."

Owen laughed and I scowled up at him. For a guy I'd just met—and a cop to boot—he wasn't making a good impression right now.

"You're laughing at me?"

"Don't fash yourself, Elspeth," he said. "It's nothing personal."

It sure felt like it.

"Are you busy now?" he added.

I gave him some serious side-eye. "Not really…"

"See up there?" He pointed to a hill that sprung

up a few blocks away. It was full of greenery and had a tower of some kind built at the top. Behind it, I could see the top of some large Greek columns. "That's Calton Hill. There's a wee monument on top and a great view of the city. Would you like to walk up there with me?"

I frowned. "Well…"

"C'mon," he said, "I'm a detective. What am I going to do?"

I glanced at the archives. "I guess I don't have anywhere to be." It didn't take much for me to cave.

Owen and I walked along the street a few blocks, then he led me up some stairs—what was with the stairs in this place?—and through some thick greenery. We passed a sign that read, *Welcome to Calton Hill*, and by the time we reached the top, I thought I was going to die. My lungs burned, giving away how unfit I actually was. Luckily for Owen, he was gracious enough not to make fun of me this time.

Before us was a large forecourt with a domed building, the tower I'd seen from below, and an unfinished copy of the *Athens Acropolis*. Literally.

Eight Greek columns were erected on one side, and two at either end. They seemed to have forgotten to finish it or maybe they had run out of money. It stood out in the open, shadowed against the sky, a mere glimpse at what it might have looked like if it'd been completed.

Owen led me across the forecourt to the side of the hill overlooking the newer part of Edinburgh. The city stretched for miles, reaching a large stretch of water, then continued to the horizon.

"See all that water? That's the Firth of Forth," Owen explained. "There are four main bridges. The Forth Bridge, Forth Road Bridge, Kincardine Bridge, and the Clackmannanshire Bridge. The Forth Bridge is the big red one, a suspension bridge, but you can't really see it from here." He grasped my shoulders and turned me towards the bustling city centre. "That's York Place down there—it's one of the main roads through the city centre. There's a nice wee art gallery there."

The wind whipped around us, buffeting my hair in all directions. I scraped it away and followed his gaze, trying to spot all the places he'd pointed out.

"What's the tower behind us?" I asked.

"That's the Nelson Monument," Owen replied. "It's a memorial for Nelson's win at the Battle of Trafalgar during the Napoleonic Wars."

"There's a lot of monuments to British people," I mused.

"Ach, don't remind us," he said with a chuckle.

Edinburgh was full of so much history, and I knew I'd barely begun to scratch the surface. Royalty like Mary Queen of Scots and many other Stuart Kings. Writers and poets like Sir Arthur Conan Doyle, Robert Burns, and Sir Walter Scott. Artists, scientists, doctors, and so many other historical figures had called this place home.

My head spun and I turned away from the view

just as a shaggy little dog ran up to us and wagged its tail. It was a wiry scrap of a thing, all black and grey with sharp brown eyes. He had no collar and no one seemed to be calling out.

I knelt down and held out my hand, palm up. "Hey, buddy," I murmured, scratching behind his ears. "Where are your people, huh?"

"Careful, I wouldn't touch it," Owen said above me.

I waved him off. "It's fine. He's friendly, see?"

Abruptly, the dog yapped and took off, bounding across the hill like a bat out of hell. I rose, bewildered at its sudden flight.

"There's been a problem with strays," Owen said, taking out his mobile phone. "I should call someone about it. Can't have the thing bothering people."

"Oh no, don't do that," I said, craning my neck to see where it'd gone. "It could belong to someone and it's just lost."

The detective snorted and his phone rang. "Seriously?" He took the call and spoke to whoever was on the other end in a clipped tone.

I turned away, more to hide the uneasiness I felt at the change in his voice more than to give him some privacy.

"*Ach*, I've been called into the station," he grumbled, stepping around so he could catch my eye. "Are you fine to make it back on your own?"

I nodded and tucked a loose strand of hair behind my ear. "Yeah, I remember the way."

He frowned and slipped his phone into his pocket. "Sorry to run, lass, but it's an emergency."

"It's your job, I understand. Thanks for the tour."

Owen smiled, the uneasiness between us fading. "You're welcome."

I lingered on top of the hill as he strode away, then jogged down the stairs, and disappeared around the corner. It was really nice of him to show me around a little, but his mood seemed to flip in an instant.

Maybe I was making it too much of a thing. *Yeah, maybe.*

Smiling to myself, I wandered towards the tower —the Nelson Monument—and found a hidden alcove that looked over the southern part of the city. Now I was out of the wind, I combed my fingers through my mousy locks and straightened my scarf.

I could see Arthur's Seat—an ancient extinct volcano—and the Old Town right up to Edinburgh Castle. With the help of a sign, I picked out the Scott Monument, the Princes Street Gardens, and the Waverley train station. A large church spire dominated the view up on the Royal Mile and I wondered what it might be.

I stood for a moment, watching the clouds swirl in the overcast sky as they dumped rain over Arthur's Seat. I was blessedly calm for the first time since I'd arrived. My father's death seemed far away, like it had happened a long time ago.

Four weeks had passed, and I was still numb—no

tears, no heartache… Was I that heartless? Was I mourning the right way? Was I morning at all?

I wiped at a stray tear and straightened my new Black Watch scarf. Maybe I did have a family tartan and just didn't know it yet. If I could know that one thing, then maybe I wouldn't feel so alone.

There. I'd said it. I was lonely.

"You shouldn't go out with that guy."

I let out a yelp and turned, coming face to face with the man who'd tried to grab me outside of Greyfriars.

The man with the dog.

5

The man stood at the end of the path, blocking my only way out.

In the daylight, I could finally see him with some clarity. Tall, sharp jaw, messy ruddy brown hair, piercing green eyes… he couldn't be a day over thirty. I took in his black overcoat—noting the hole in one elbow—and his grey knitted jumper, black jeans, and heavy black combat boots.

He was the complete opposite of Owen.

"*You,*" I snarled, overcome with a wave of anger which surprised me. "*Get out of my way.*"

He held up his hands. "I just need to talk to you, that's all."

"I'll have you know that I reported you to the police."

"Don't fash yourself," he told me.

"Fash?" I exclaimed. "What is fash? Everyone is

telling me not to do it like I'm five years old! I assume it means worry, but I will worry!"

"Ach," he said, scratching his head. "You're a little worked up there, lass. You ought to calm yourself a wee bit. I'm not trying to abduct you."

"Then don't go around grabbing women's arms and dragging them into the shadows," I hissed, taking a step towards the fence. It was the only way I could go.

"I was *trying to help you*," he said.

My hands curled around the bars behind me. "I don't believe you."

The man frowned and ran his hand through his hair. It was clear he wasn't used to being told no. Well, looking like *that*, I supposed women lined up around the block just for the chance to hear him say whatever he wanted to them.

"Perhaps I should introduce myself. Raurich 'Rory' Mackenzie," he said, bowing with a flourish, "at your service."

I snorted.

"This is the part where you tell me your name," he prodded.

"*Not on your life.*"

His frown deepened and he shook his head.

"Why are you hanging around that guy? Can't you see what he is?" He hesitated, then jabbed a finger at me. "You're with him, aren't you? That's why I've never seen you around here."

"Of course, I'm not from around here," I stated. "I'm *Australian*."

"Who are you?" His eyes widened. "Are you from the homeland?"

"The what?" I inched backwards, looking for an escape route. "I'm sorry, but I can't help you. I don't know anything about drugs or homelands. That guy I was with? He's a police officer. A *detective*."

"Can it be possible?" he whispered, staring at me in shock. "Aye, it is... *You don't know*."

"Know what?" I demanded.

"You're a Druid," he said. "I can literally feel the Colour bleeding from your skin. No wonder that guy is after you. You're completely out of control."

"I'm out of control?" I raged. "You're high!"

"I wouldn't be rational if I was high."

"And everything you just said, that's what you call rational? Well, *Rory*, I call it a drug-induced hallucination and I won't have any part of it!"

This entire place was crazy. I need to go to the airport and get out of here as soon as possible. I don't need to know about my dad's past if this was the trouble it brought. I was going to go home and get a job in retail.

"It's the truth," he said. "You have to believe me."

"I don't have to do anything." My gaze flickered to the path, but there was still no way around him.

"They want to take your Colour," he said, growing more erratic. "Can't you see?"

I narrowed my eyes. "If you're telling the truth, you'll let me go."

"I can't. It's not safe for you. They know who you are now."

At that moment, a group of people emerged at the end of the path, bustling into the alcove.

"Help!" I cried, lunging towards them.

Rory grabbed my arm and wrenched me back before I could rush past him. I faltered as the people didn't react—not one person looked in our direction. They laughed amongst themselves and huddled around the fence, pointing at the view of Edinburgh behind us.

"Hey!" I shouted again. "Listen to me!"

"They can't see or hear us," Rory said, holding my arm. "You can scream all you like, but no one will hear."

My hands shook and the same panic I felt last night began to rise. "I don't understand. I-I…"

"Like I said. You're a Druid. *Like me.*"

Confusion clouded my mind and I didn't know what to do. I stood there, frozen in the spot, hovering somewhere between terror and hopelessness.

"Now that I have your attention," Rory said, standing beside me, "can we please have a rational conversation?"

I opened my mouth, but nothing came out.

"We don't have much time," he went on. "I used too much Colour and they've likely noticed."

"Colour?" I blinked. Everything he said confused the hell out of me.

"It's what we call our powers," he explained. "The Colour of nature."

"Powers?" I shook my head. "I have no powers. I'm not special."

"You still want to believe that after what you just witnessed?" Rory looked a little frustrated, but there was a lot of that going around.

"You did that, not me."

"So you believe me?" He didn't look convinced.

"This isn't happening to me," I muttered to myself. "*This isn't real.*"

Rory laid his hand on my shoulder. "There's more to this reality than anyone will ever realise. There are nightmares that don't bear mentioning, but there are also things that are made from beautiful magic. The human world is just a thin layer on the surface of so much more."

Calmness spread through me like a wave of warmth from the sun on a bright, spring day. For a moment, I almost believed him. What if there was more? What if this was what my dad was hiding from me? If that was true, then there must've been something dangerous enough for him to take me all the way to Australia.

I shook my head and knocked Rory's hand away. "I can't. This stuff... It's children's stories, not real life."

No doubt there were people out there who wished

they could escape their lives into something otherworldly, but I wasn't one of them. I believed in science and rational thinking. I believed in *evidence*.

"Ach, and she thinks I'm the one who's doolally," Rory muttered.

"What did you just say about me?" I demanded, but he didn't reply.

He stood in front of me and held open his hand. For a moment I was confused, then shock began to set in as a blue shimmering light sparked in the centre of his hand…and began to grow.

Lines sprouted, forming corners and angles, growing and becoming more complex as they folded back on themselves. Along the thread, the colour merged from blue to purple to green and beyond.

It was a shimmering geometric, holographic cube.

"It's the beginning of a prism," Rory explained. "Weave one of these and you can manifest just about anything."

"And you're saying I can do this?"

He nodded, completely serious. "Care to tell me your name now, lass?"

"Elspeth," I whispered, staring at the shimmering shape in his palm. "My name is Elspeth."

"There aren't many of us in this world, but those who are… Well, we know them all, Elspeth. But you?" He studied my features and shook his head. "I've never seen you before."

"I don't know what to tell you," I whispered as he closed his hand, cutting off the light.

"Who are your parents? What did they do?"

"My father was an environmental scientist."

"Was?" He tilted his head to the side. "Did he die in a car accident? They usually do in these stories."

"He died a hero," I snarled. "Don't you go saying things like to that. You didn't know him."

He held up his hands and took a step back. "All right, all right. I never said the man wasn't good. Dare I ask about your mother?"

"I don't know who she was. Dad never spoke about her."

He was silent for a moment as the group of people wandered past, leaving us alone in the alcove once more.

"Well, one thing's clear," he murmured. "If you're determined to walk around Edinburgh, you need to learn how to hide yourself."

"Hide myself?" I echoed.

"That's how they found you last night. If I wasn't there…" He shook his head.

The man with the pointed teeth? I screwed my face up, confused. Who were 'they' exactly?

"Will you come with me?" Rory took my hand and caught my gaze. "Please?"

I hesitated, conflicted between what I'd seen since arriving in Scotland and what I knew reality ought to be.

Still, this could be my chance to find out the truth about who I was and where I'd come from, but at what cost? I wasn't special. I didn't have any magical powers or mysterious connection with nature. I was just a plain woman with no family.

I pulled my hand away.

How could I go with him? He could be luring me into a trap or worse. Maybe I was being conned and was about to fall headfirst into a human trafficking ring.

Rory had shown me a few tricks, but it wasn't enough to convince me that magic was real. Those people could have been actors and that light in his hand could have been a projection or hologram of some sort. He'd already tried to snatch me once.

"No," I said, shaking my head.

"Elspeth," he urged, "you must come with me. It's not safe."

"This is just… It's not enough." I stepped around him and he didn't try to stop me. I walked away, emerging out of the alcove into a changed world.

While I was talking to Rory, the hill had fallen silent. Rain began to fall, driving away the last of the tourists and I was alone at what felt like the top of the world—or the end of it.

What do I do now? I wasn't sure if I wanted to continue my search, let alone stay in Scotland. Maybe I should go get my things and get on the next train to London. It was easy enough to change my plans. Everything was booked, just the dates needed to be rearranged.

"Elspeth!" Owen's voice rang out across the forecourt and I turned to find him jogging towards me. "I'm glad you're still here," he said, stopping in front of me. "Turned out that call was a false alarm."

I stared at him, remembering what Rory had said. *Why are you hanging around that guy? Can't you see what he is?* I blinked as droplets of misty water settled on my eyelashes.

Something didn't feel right. Suddenly, I was aware that my fingers ached and I closed my hands into tight fists.

Owen's brow creased and he stepped closer. "Elspeth? What's wrong?"

"I-I don't feel so good," I muttered, looking for a bench. I needed to sit before I fainted.

He reached for me. "Here, let me help you."

The moment he touched my skin, the world splintered and a burst of colour shot through my vision. I gasped and recoiled when I saw the creature looking down at me.

It wasn't handsome Owen Murray, the police detective who I was supposed to trust. It was a greyish-skinned man with black eyes and...*pointed teeth.*

"You're—" The words died in my mouth as the vision faded. I blinked once more and Owen's human face was the one glaring at me.

He grabbed my arm and dragged me against his body with a snarl, his fingers biting into my skin.

"Owen, what are you doing?" I demanded, pulling against his grasp. "*Let me go.*"

"I've got no patience for this pathetic game," he rasped. "You're coming with me."

Terror threatened to overwhelm me like it had the night before, but I wasn't going to let it turn me into a useless lump this time. I opened my mouth to scream, but I wasn't prepared for the word that came out of it.

"Rory!" I screeched, digging my heels into the grass, pulling against Owen's grasp with everything I had. "*Rory!*"

A black blur shot across the hill and an enormous German Shepard leapt into the air towards Owen, its jaws snapping. It latched onto his arm and shook, dislodging the hand holding my arm.

I fell, landing hard on my arse as Owen shouted and fought the dog. His face began to change, flickering wildly between human and monster, and I scrambled backwards, trying to get away.

Hands hooked underneath my arms and I was hauled to my feet. Spinning, I lashed out only for Rory to catch my forearm before my fist could collide with his face.

"It's only me," he said. "Hold your horses, lass." He wrapped his arm around my waist and drew me away from Owen.

The dog yelped as the detective kicked it in the ribs and broke free. He turned towards us, his eyes black and full of a palpable rage that crackled across the hill.

"Elspeth..." Rory grasped my hand and began to back away, "now would be the perfect time to run."

6

———

My heart felt like it was going to burst as Rory and I ran from Calton Hill.

Behind us, I could hear Owen's boots thunder against the stone path in pursuit, the dog nowhere to be see.

We burst out onto the footpath, almost colliding with a cluster of pedestrians. Rory guided me to the right, back towards the archives and the city centre.

I threw a glance over my shoulder and caught sight of Owen shoving his way through a group of tourists waiting outside a hotel.

That's why I wasn't looking when Rory abruptly dragged me across the road…right into the path of a double decker bus.

I screamed, but the driver never saw us as Rory pulled me up onto the footpath, the wall of metal and glass brushing past as it continued its route like we hadn't been there at all. The people waiting at the pedestrian crossing hadn't noticed, either.

Rory wasn't waiting around to see if we'd lost Owen. He tugged my hand and we ran towards the North Bridge, weaving between the throng of people walking to and from the Old Town.

"Why can't anyone see us?" I called after him.

"We're surrounded by an illusion," he replied. "I'll explain it all later, okay?" *If there was going to be a later.*

We slowed to a fast walk and I almost had to break into a jog to keep up with Rory's long stride.

What was I doing? This wasn't me. I was shy and awkward to the extreme. Why would they want someone like me?

"*Ach*, he's right behind us," Rory hissed. I threw a glance over my shoulder, but he tugged my arm. "Don't look back. Just keep going."

"Why aren't we running? This seems like a running moment."

"There's too many people. We risk revealing ourselves to the humans. If we have a chance to get away without fighting, I'm going to take it."

"*Fighting?*"

"Aye."

I wasn't in a position to challenge his assessment, so I followed him across the bridge.

Historic buildings and the remnants of ancient volcanoes dominated the view from both sides, and on any other day, I would have paused to take it all in, but I was aware of the monster following in our footsteps.

On the other side of the bridge, the *Scotsman Hotel* reared up on the right and various shops dominated the ground floor of the *Hilton Hotel* on the left. The façades were all greyish brown, the stone discoloured from age and pollution. A few copper domes and roofs dotted here and there, the glossy orange long oxidised into green.

Rory led me onto the Royal Mile just as the rain began to change from an annoying mist into fully formed droplets.

We weaved past walking tour groups who were regaled with ghost stories and tales of the filthy and overpopulated state the city used to endure in the sixteenth century. Rory jostled past slow walkers and groups of people milling about outside souvenir shops.

His grip tightened on my hand. "Down here."

We slipped into one of the closes that ran off the main road. I'd read in Mrs. Campbell's information display folder that the closes used to be gated alleyways which led to private property, but as the city grew and modernised, they were left open as thoroughfares for foot traffic.

This one made a sharp decline down the northern side of the hill the Old Town sat on—the steep grade broken up by a few sporadic sets of stairs.

About halfway down the hill, Rory pulled me into an alcove that was barely big enough for the both of us, let alone big enough to conceal our presence from Owen…or whatever he was.

We were under the eave of a door that looked like it hadn't seen any use for a long time. Rory pressed his palms on either side of the jamb, shielding me with his body. The air shimmered behind him and I blinked, wondering if he'd just used his powers to hide us.

I didn't know why, but I trusted him. When Owen grabbed me, it was Rory who I called to for help. That had to mean something.

I'd barely had enough time to catch my breath since we'd run from Calton Hill. Now that we'd stopped, everything rushed back. The moment Owen had me in his grasp, then the German Shepard appearing out of nowhere and clamping its vice-like jaws down on his arm.

"What happened to your dog?" I whispered as we huddled in the shadows.

"That's not a dog," Rory replied. "That's Jaimie Fraser!"

I blinked. "What, from that Outlander TV show?"

"It was a series of books before it was ever a television programme, I'll have you know," he declared with a pout. "I call him that because the lassies swoon when you tell them you named your dog after a dashing romantic hero."

"That's such a male thing to say."

"You're very wry for a lass who just escaped an attempted abduction. How many times is that now?"

"I've lost count." I peered down the close, but couldn't see anyone—or anything—coming in either direction. "But aren't you worried about leaving your dog to wander the city alone?"

Rory snorted. "Jaimie Fraser can handle himself," he told me. "Don't fash about him."

He gestured for me to be quiet and I bit my tongue, my heartbeat speeding up. The close was barely wide enough for two people to stand side by side. If I reached out, I could almost touch the opposite wall. A low doorway at the top of the stairs was set into the house, and above the mantle was an echo of Edinburgh's past etched in Medieval script. *Lord be merciful to me.* Though the letter 'u' in merciful, was carved as a 'v'.

A chill passed through my body at the omen. Rory pressed against me, lending me his warmth…but I wasn't cold.

"Why don't you fight him?" I whispered into Rory's ear.

"I'm not prepared to take down a Chimera in broad daylight," he told me. "Besides, this one is strong. I've never felt power like his before."

"A Chimera?"

"The Chimera are a legion of Dark Fae," he said as if talking about fairies was the most ordinary thing in the world. "They like to hunt Druids for their power. That guy, your precious detective, was grooming you in order to steal your power."

I gasped. "He what?"

"Once he had it, he would have killed you."

I tensed and my heartbeat increased to a full gallop. There was so much I didn't understand about what was happening, but kill was a notion that doesn't need much brain power to comprehend. *Owen wanted to kill me.*

I felt sick.

"It doesn't matter who you are or where you came from," Rory murmured. "You're a Druid, Elspeth, and I will protect you. *It's that simple.*"

He tensed abruptly, his jaw twitching. I peered underneath his arm and saw Owen prowling down the close, his boots scraping against the flagstones. He sauntered down one flight of stairs, then inched closer to where we were hidden, sniffing the air.

"I know you're here, Druid," the detective said. "There's no use hiding… I can do this all day if we have to."

I looked up at Rory. His jaw was tense, and his eyes were brimming with anger. He'd have to fight him, and he wasn't pleased about it. I shook my head slightly, but he'd already seemed to have resigned himself to the fact.

"Elspeth, whatever happens…stay behind me."

"But you said—"

"It's going to be okay." He pulled a large knife from underneath his coat and flipped it over in his hand with a flourish. The air shimmered as he stepped out of the alcove and stood before Owen.

"I won't go down without a fight, just so you know," he said to the detective.

"I wouldn't expect anything less, but you could save yourself a lot of pain by just giving me the girl."

I huddled in the alcove, watching as rain beat down on the two men in a steady stream. It was quite the feat of nature, considering how narrow the close was, but the closer I looked, the more I could see the droplets skim off Rory's shoulders like an invisible forcefield hovered around him.

Owen smirked and strode towards the Druid as water ran down his face and soaked his clothes.

Rory flipped the knife in his hand and struck, the blade hissing through the air. The detective moved like lightning, grabbed his wrist and pounded his fist into the Druid's stomach.

The knife fell from Rory's grasp. It clattered along the stone walkway, tumbled down the stairs, and landed at my feet.

The fight that came next happened so fast, I could hardly follow it. Rory broke free and landed a punch to Owen's cheek that sent a strange vibration through the air. My stomach rolled as the detective pushed the Druid against the wall and cracked the younger man's head against the stone.

Rory kneed Owen between the legs, causing him to double over, then clipped him in the face with another power-laden punch, but the detective recovered from each blow too quickly for him to keep up.

Now I understood why Rory didn't want to fight him. Owen was too strong.

The detective swept Rory's feet from underneath him and the Druid fell hard on his back, hitting his head as he went down.

My hand flew to my mouth and the same terror I felt the night before came flooding back.

My gaze met Rory's as Owen's hand clamped around his neck. I stared in horror as his skin began to turn blue as the detective—the *Chimera*—crushed his windpipe and cut off his air supply.

I could see the words he couldn't say etched in his eyes. *Run.*

He wanted me to get away but I couldn't leave him, not after he'd told me what the Chimera did to people. Owen would take his power, then kill him.

Darting out of the alcove and into the rain, I snatched up the knife and brandished it at the detective. "*Let him go.*"

He stood, his grasp slipping away from Rory's neck, but the younger man didn't move.

Owen stood at the top of the stairs, smirking down at me, clearly confident he was going to win despite me being the one who was holding the blade.

"Put down the knife, Elspeth," he said. "It's over. Don't make this harder than it has to be."

I jutted out my chin in defiance. "I'm not going to let you kill us."

"Kill you?" he scoffed. "Who said anything about killing?"

"I don't believe you." I tightened my grip on the knife, vowing to stab him if he got any closer.

"What lies has that Druid filled your head with, Elspeth?" Owen crooned. "Your power is useless without you to wield it. I just want to help you understand."

My gaze fell to Rory, who was barely holding onto consciousness. *They were both telling me the same thing…*

"Give me the knife, Elspeth," Owen urged. "Come with me and I will give you all the answers you deserve. *I can tell you about your parents.*"

I hesitated, his words striking me where it mattered the most.

"Elspeth…" he stepped closer, "this is all just a huge misunderstanding."

I shook my head, thinking about everything he'd told me…and everything Rory had.

The man at Greyfriars hadn't been trying to help me, but Rory and his mysterious dog had been there to stop him. Owen had been rather eager to help me when I'd gone into the police station. Then he'd conveniently ran into me outside the archives.

All Rory had tried to do was try to convince me I was in danger.

"I'm not going anywhere with you," I snarled at Owen.

"So you're choosing without fully understanding what you're giving away," he mused in a disappointed tone. "So be it."

"I will attack you in self-defence," I warned.

He laughed like I'd just told the funniest joke ever. "I have all the power here, Elspeth. Even if you get away, I have the resources of the Scottish police at my back. What do you have?"

"CCTV," I hissed. "Evidence. *Testimony*. You're crooked, Owen, and soon everyone will know."

Owen laughed and shook his head. "The Druid already took care of the evidence for me. Leave them conscious enough for their illusions to hold and no one will hear you scream."

I took a step back, holding the knife higher.

"You could run, but it would only be a matter of time before you were caught," he went on. "You have no family, no connections, and no clue what you're doing. If you try to go home, your passport will be flagged and you'll be detained. You won't be able to leave the country."

Think, Elspeth. Think. Rory said I was a Druid, so I must have something I could fight back with. But how in the world did I find it?

Owen crept down the stairs. "She's going to try to fight," he mused. "*Interesting.*"

"Stay away from me," I warned.

"You're alone, Elspeth. No one is coming to save you. You have nothing. You are *nobody*."

I trembled, a vision of my father being consumed by a firestorm flashed through my mind. Arms and claws twisted through the blaze, tearing at his bright yellow uniform, searing the flesh from his bones.

Tears fell from my eyes and the knife trembled in my hand.

Owen hesitated, his stride faltering…but it was only for a split-second. He lunged, going for the knife, and I stabbed towards him with a cry.

What happened next felt like slow motion. A blue flame enveloped the blade as it sank into Owen's chest and his eyes widened in shock. Light exploded around us—its source unknown—and bounced off the walls of the buildings on either side of us.

Owen collapsed to his knees and the mask hiding his true nature slipped. Grey flesh bled through his Caucasian colouring and pitch-black eyes stared up at me as his mouth gaped, revealing his pointed teeth.

"You killed him, didn't you?" I demanded. *"You killed my father."*

"It wasn't me," Owen rasped.

"But it was one of you."

All the pain, grief, and suffering I'd been bottling up erupted like a volcano. I twisted the knife, roaring my agony as thick, congealed blood seeped from Owen's chest…and something inside me broke free.

Something powerful and unknown.

Something terrible.

Electricity sparked, connecting me to everything —the sky, the wind, the rain… The moss growing on the walls. The grass sprouting in the gardens at the bottom of the hill. The pigeons bustling around St. Giles Cathedral up on the Royal Mile. The tourists walking to and fro, shopping for tacky souvenirs. Even

Rory, who was trying to fight off the intoxicating pull of unconsciousness.

And I felt the presence of Owen Murray…*Chimera*.

Coloured spikes burst out of my arm, crystallising as they shot into the knife and into the Fae who kneeled before me. Light pulsed and became so blinding that everything went dark…and the life tore from my veins.

7

———

When I opened my eyes, I found myself in an unfamiliar bed. Thankfully, I was fully clothed—apart from my boots, scarf, and jacket.

A fire crackled in an open fireplace, the warm glow lighting the room. The mingled smells of smoke and freshly spilt wood filled the room with a homely scent, and I sat up.

The black German Shepard was stretched out on the end of the bed, its eyes glowing in the firelight.

I stared at it for a moment before it lifted its head and looked at me.

"Woof," it said.

I cried out in alarm as the extremely human sounding word rolled out of the dog's mouth.

The door burst open and Rory came charging in. He narrowed his eyes when he saw the dog.

"Jaimie Fraser," he scolded, *"we've talked about this."*

The dog pushed off the bed with a sigh and sat

before the fireplace…then began to change. Its spine bulged and grew, its hair shrank back into its flesh, and its snout changed into something human-like.

A mixture of shock, awe, and a little disgust overcame me as I clutched the blanket to my chest. Rory's dog was turning into a man. A rather large, muscular, *naked* man.

He stood as the last of his animal fur faded— but still left behind a rather furry human chest— and grinned down at me. Taller than Rory by a whole head, his curly black hair fell into his eyes and he wore a full beard to match his wild Scotsman look.

"Ach," Rory said, throwing a pillow at the man's nether regions, "the lass doesn't want to see your bits, Jaimie."

"What's the matter, lass?" the dog-man named Jaimie asked in an accent thicker than any I'd heard so far. "Never seen a willy before, aye?"

I snorted and laughed. I was in a dream…or a comedy. A tragic comedy.

"Ach, *lass*," Jaimie complained.

"A wee willy," Rory said with a laugh. "Get out, you eejit."

Jaimie cursed and waddled from the room, holding the pillow over his 'wee willy', but forgot about the full moon bringing up the rear.

Rory kicked the door closed with the toe of his boot and threw another log onto the fire. Sparks crackled and embers flew up into the chimney and I almost heard my father's voice echo to me from within the flame.

"I'm glad you're awake…and in one piece," Rory said, sitting on the end of the bed.

My gaze flicked to the door. "Can-can you do that?"

"No," he replied, "it's a rare skill. There are only a few of us who can shapeshift."

"All this time, your dog was a man?"

"He's not my dog, so to speak," he told me. "We're a team more often than not."

I lowered my gaze and stared at my hand. Flexing my fingers, I felt something ripple beneath the surface and quickly shoved it underneath the blanket.

Rory watched me with a furrowed brow.

"Where are we?" I asked.

"This is my room," he replied. "We have a house on the Mile. It's hidden by illusions, so don't fash."

Rory's room? I looked around again but didn't see anything out of the ordinary. There weren't any magic wands, potions, or robes anywhere. Though somehow, I was sure Druids didn't work like the wizards out of a *Harry Potter* novel.

My boots sat on the floor and my jacket, scarf, and bag lay on a rickety old chair.

"You wanted to know if you had powers," he said. "Well, you popped the cork off that bottle and sent it flying to the moon and back. You went supernova, lass."

"Supernova?" Was that a technical term? *No, I don't think so.*

"You shook the windows. Scared the shite out of me."

A vision of Owen on his knees before me with the knife in his chest appeared in my mind. "Did…did I kill him?"

Rory frowned. "No, unfortunately not."

I didn't want to take someone's life but it was a double-edged sword. Owen was deeply intrenched in the Scottish police, his façade so well-honed no one would question any tactics he used to get to Rory…and me.

I worried the edge of the blanket. "I just made a whole lot of trouble for you, didn't I?"

"Aye, but it is what it is."

"I'm sorry," I blurted. "I didn't know. About any of it."

"Don't fash yourself, Elspeth." A scratching at the door pulled Rory's attention and he muttered under his breath, "Ach, what is it now?"

He wrenched open the door and cursed in what sounded like Gaelic.

A large tabby cat sprung up onto the bed and sat beside me, its green eyes narrowing as it inspected me. It had to be at least twice the size of a normal house cat, but it was stunning. Its black stripes were mixed with brown and ginger fur, its whiskers were long and spiky, and its nose perfectly pink.

I reached out to scratch it on the head but pulled back at the last moment. "Is that another person?"

"No, that's just a cat, but there are strings attached with every animal you see with us." He kicked the door closed and the fire flickered.

"Strings?"

"Delilah likes to save fragmented souls and give them new life," Rory explained like it was a normal thing to do. "They used to be human, but for some reason their souls were damaged or broken. Coming back as a cat is better than floating in nothing for eternity."

"What about the cat?"

He tilted his head to the side. "What about it?"

"Well...doesn't it mind that it's sharing it's body with someone else?"

Rory laughed. "They're not actual animals. They're constructs."

"Constructs?"

He nodded and took my hand, guiding it towards the tabby cat. "Made of Colour so thick, no one can tell the difference between flesh and prism."

My fingers threaded through the cat's hair and it purred. It narrowed its eyes as it kneaded the blanket with its claws.

"This is a new one," Rory added. "Can you see how its fur sparkles?"

I ran my fingers through the cat's fur and it rolled onto its back, letting me tickle its belly—a rarity for a feline with claws as sharp as the ones currently kneading the air.

"I want to believe," I whispered, tears gathering in my eyes, "but…"

"You don't think you deserve it, do you?" Rory frowned. "Why not?"

Despair overcame me and I kicked my legs out of bed. I snatched up my socks and hopped on one foot, desperately trying to pull them onto my feet.

"I can't stay here," I said. "I've got a train ticket to London."

He snorted and rolled his eyes. "What do you want to go to that heaving cesspool for? The only good thing to come out of England is the road to Scotland."

"Heathrow," I snapped, not knowing if I should be offended on the English's behalf—even though I was Scottish myself. *Scottish with an Australian accent.* "Heathrow is in London and there's a plane seat with my name on it. I had it all planned out."

"Oh, so now you're running away from reality. That's a healthy way to deal with life's challenges."

"You call a talking dog, a monster who plays dress up, a cat with a human soul, and exploding magical powers one of *life's challenges*? You're deluded." I shoved my feet into my boots and snatched up my jacket.

Rory watched me with infuriating amusement. "By your reasoning, you're the one who's deluded, Elspeth."

I turned. "Excuse me?"

"Well, you're the one who's seeing things, after all." He grinned at me and I felt a sudden urge to punch the smirk right off his stupid face.

"The two faces of Rory Mackenzie," I drawled. "One's a sweet man and the other is a raging arsehole!"

"Raging arsehole?" he exclaimed. "After all I risked saving you from that Chimera scum, you're calling *me* a raging arsehole?"

"Is that even your real name? I didn't know Scottish Highland clans were full of *Druids*."

"No, I'm not a true Mackenzie, but it doesn't matter," he spluttered. "We're talking about you, Elspeth."

"If we're talking about who saved who, then it's me you should thank!"

"So you're admitting it, then? You are a Druid, Elspeth, and wherever you go, the Chimera will follow. They know who you are now, and it doesn't matter if you're willing to accept it or not."

My knees shook and I bit my bottom lip. I was a mess. *Everything* was a mess.

"But my dad was an environmental scientist," I murmured, my voice wavering. "He was…"

"Well, someone was a Druid," Rory said. "I don't want to speculate, but I think we should focus on you right now. The family tree can come later."

I shook my head and lowered my gaze so my tangled hair covered my face.

"Ach, you stubborn lass."

"If I believe it, then it's true," I shouted at him. "*They murdered my father.*"

The bed rattled and scraped across the floor an inch, causing the cat to rise. It hissed and flicked its tail back and forth.

"Careful," Rory warned. "I don't want a repeat performance."

I didn't know this world existed, let alone my father being a part of it. He was more than my dad—he was my best friend. We knew everything about one another, us against the world, but now I realise I don't know the first thing about him.

"They killed him," I whispered, my jacket slipping from my fingers and hit the floor with a dull thud. "They pulled him into the fire and…"

"Likely they *were* the fire," Rory murmured.

I wiped at my tears. "What?"

"Elemental warriors. There aren't many of them on Earth, but they have a pact with the Chimera. They sought their protection in exchange for some nefarious duties of their own."

"Bounty hunting."

He nodded. "I'm sorry, I didn't know."

Neither did I.

"Elspeth, I'm not here to hurt you." Rory's thumb pressed against my wrist and the warmth spread, calling to the strange power that had exploded on the street. "I want to help."

My breath caught as I felt the same unfamiliar

energy rise. Fear began to quicken my heart and I pulled against Rory's hold.

The cat yowled and spat, causing him to let me go.

"Okay, okay, you whining flea bag," he said to it. "No funny business." He raised an eyebrow at me. "It seems like you've got yourself a cat."

"A cat?" I exclaimed. "What am I going to do with a cat?"

Rory laughed and shook his head, saying something in Gaelic.

"What?" I demanded. "What does that mean?"

"It means, the cat is the least of your problems." *The Chimera.*

"They'll be hunting me now, won't they?" I whispered. "I'm… I…"

"This is what I know," Rory said, tugging me back onto the bed. "You came here looking for answers about your father's family and found out the truth wasn't so magical as you had expected. You *are* special, Elspeth, but it's rarely the key to eternal happiness."

"With power comes responsibility," I murmured.

"*Exactly.*"

I shook my head. "What do I do now?"

"I can't tell you want to do," Rory told me. "But if you want my opinion…"

"I'm so lost." The cat rose its head and peered at me. "I don't know a single thing about this world or what I did out there. I don't know who I'm supposed to be."

"Well, acknowledgement is the first step of acceptance."

I wasn't taking the bait, not after everything that had happened. Another argument wouldn't help anybody.

"There's Jaimie Fraser the dog-man, and you mentioned someone named Delilah." His girlfriend most likely, which made our current position totally awkward. There was no way a guy who looked like Rory Mackenzie was unattached…or interested in a plain Jane like me. "How many Druids are there?"

"Not many, but enough," he replied, keeping it vague. "Which is why I'm confused about you. Hiding a Druid child? It's nigh on impossible."

But my father did it. *Why?*

Rory sensed my turmoil and took my hands in his. "Look, it's a shock. You've believed you were human your entire life and now everything has changed. I don't understand what you're going through, but I can help you understand what it is you've fallen into. That's what I promised you, remember?"

I nodded, remembering our conversation on top of Calton Hill.

"Can I tell you our story?" he asked. "The story of the Druids?"

"Yes…" I swallowed hard. "I'd like that." And I owed it to him after all the trouble I'd put him through.

"Once, the Druids lived in a world of peace and beauty," he began. "A world rich in nature. A world where we lived in harmony. We call it the Druid homeland—*Thríbhís Mhór*."

"What language is that?"

"It is old Irish for the three spiralled triskele." He picked up my hand and drew the pattern on my palm, a blue glow forming where he touched. "It is the connection between earth, sea, and sky." The glow faded, leaving behind a tingling sensation. "Thousands of years ago, the Druids became restless and opened portals to other realities, forging a path as explorers of space and time. One of those realities was Earth, but not this one."

"Another Earth?" I murmured.

"Yes. Similar, but different in so many small ways," he explained. "It was there we forged an alliance with another supernatural species, but it ended in calamity. Their own meddling opened a rift in the fabric of the universe, allowing a horde of Dark creatures to stream through. In the years that followed, the Druids were hunted almost to extinction. Knowing there was no way we could stop the Darkness from spreading, our leader Merlin decided to guide our people home. Our wandering would be over, and we could begin anew in our ancestral lands. Our exploration was folly."

"Merlin?" I asked. "*The* Merlin from the stories about Camelot?"

Rory nodded. "It was a real place, in another world."

I shivered, his story caused goosebumps to prickle over my exposed skin. Was he telling me the truth? I wasn't sure I could deny the things he was telling me anymore. For better or worse, I believed him.

"To escape," he continued, "Merlin led our people through the Darklands, the reality surrounding *Thríbhís Mhór*. It was a dangerous journey and our people became separated. The only way we could survive the nightmarish landscape was to open a portal to another reality." He sighed and looked at the fire. "That's how we came to this world."

"Only to be hunted again." My heart ached and I pressed the heel of my palm against my chest.

"This Earth had its own share of problems," he added. "Its own wars, its own supernatural creatures, its own version of humanity…and we landed in the middle of another battle. One we were able to stay out of until recently."

"You talk about it like you were there," I mused.

"Druids live a long time, but I was born here," Rory said with a chuckle. "This happened about eight hundred years ago."

"That long? Why can't you go home?"

He shrugged. "We don't know the way."

"And the Fae? They are the other supernatural race?"

"The Fae have their own complicated story, and not all of them are bad. There are some good ones out there, but they rarely leave Ireland. It's been that way for thousands of years. They have portals to their realm, but they are now guarded by the Witches. They have their own struggles, too."

"Witches? First Druids, then Fae, and now Witches?"

Rory snorted. "Like I said, *it's complicated.*"

"I'll say. I'm still confused."

"You'll figure it out. You did manage to use your Colour at least, so that's a good start."

Colour. Magical powers. That was who I was? How didn't I know? Crystals of light had splintered out of my arm—there was no way I was unseeing *that.*

It was clear I had a lot to learn. Rory could help me figure out what it meant to be a Druid, and maybe his people would know my father…and maybe my mother.

And home—

"My passport," I said with a groan. "My things are still at Mrs. Campbell's." She was such a busybody, it was likely she'd already reported me missing.

"Is a passport really that important?" Rory asked.

"It is if I want to go home."

"The Chimera know where you were staying," he told me. "If you go back there, they'll find you again. No doubt the apartments are being watched, or if 'Detective' Owen has gathered his wits, it's already been cleaned out by the police."

I hesitated. "How long *have* I been here?

"Only a night."

Only? Three days in Edinburgh and I'd been attacked on the street, chased by a Fae, groomed by a crooked detective, stabbed a guy in the chest, and literally exploded. Not to mention the alternate realities, shapeshifting men, and portal-guarding Irish Witches.

"After what you've seen here, do you really want to go back to Australia?" Rory asked. "To a normal life?"

"I don't know what I want to do," I replied truthfully. "I've just had the motherlode of all info-dumps upended on my broken life. I've barely had time to grieve my father's death. In the spirit of transparency, I've been avoiding it."

Rory looked troubled and glanced at the cat. "You can go if that's what you want, but not until you learn how to protect yourself…and dampen your Colour."

"What about my things?"

He sighed and stroked the cat's back. "I'll go with you. Can't have you running out of clean pants. It would be a *cat*astrophe."

8

Turned out, 'pants' was the UK's way of referring to underpants.

Rory's house—or at least the room he had in a share house with several other Druids, including the dog-man Jaimie—wasn't far from *Mrs. Campbell's Serviced Apartments*. Still, Rory took a slow path down the hill towards Holyrood.

The Mile was bustling with tourists and locals. All the shops were open, spilling warm, inviting light onto the footpath. A bagpiper stood on a corner, dressed in a traditional uniform made up of a kilt, sash, hat, and waistcoat. He played a loud, droning tune that sounded familiar, but I didn't know what it was called.

"Ach, it's quiet," Rory said, oblivious to the jarring sound of the bagpipes. "I expected more fuss after what you did."

"Should we be out?" I asked, staying close to his side. "I mean, I'd like my stuff, but it can wait."

"We're well hidden," he told me. "If we don't use any Colours or make direct eye contact with the Fae, then we're safe enough."

"But doesn't your illusion use Colour?"

"Technically yes, but not enough for anyone to notice. For now, we blend in so if any Fae notices us, they can't tell the difference."

"Just two humans out for a stroll?"

"See?" He knocked his elbow against my arm. "You're adjusting to the covert life already."

In that moment, I realised I liked him. *A lot*. We barely knew one another, but it didn't matter. The only other person who I'd ever been able to speak this freely with was Dad.

My heart twisted at the thought of my father. There'd be time for questions and answers later. If he was a Druid, then someone here ought to have known him.

I glanced at Rory and attempted to puzzle him out, but it was impossible. He seemed like the kind of guy to hide his true emotions behind sarcasm and charm, but he'd come through on all of his promises —in a roundabout way. He was one of those rare unicorns who did exactly what they said they were going to do.

"Why are you helping me?" I asked.

"Here comes your hourly existential crisis," he mused.

"*I'm serious.*"

He shrugged. "You're a Druid and Druids help

their own."

"Is it really that simple?" I wondered out loud.

"It's that simple."

I decided to take it with a grain of salt—everybody wanted something, even if they said otherwise. Trust for trust, like for like.

"Rory? What do the Chimera want with Druid powers?"

"We're a unique species in this world," he replied. "What we wield is different from elemental forces the Witches do. We go much deeper than earth, air, fire, and water. Druids can open portals."

"The Witches guard the Fae portals in Ireland," I noted, "but the Chimera can't open their own?"

"No, not from here, and especially not without permission. They're bound by covenants within their own species, but we are not."

"They want to come and go as they please…"

"And break free of their own shackles." He sighed and guided me around a group of slow walkers. "The Chimera have been here for centuries. A thousand years at least. Until the Witches reopened the portals, they were nothing but withered husks, trapped within the confines of Ireland."

"So, they couldn't survive without access to the power that came through the portals?" Like a phone without a charger…or a solar panel without the sun.

"They can't survive long term away from their own world," he replied. "Now the portals are open, and they have their full strength back." I wondered how long 'long term' meant to a Fae if they'd been here for a thousand years.

"So with the link restored, they came back to life with a vengeance."

Rory snorted, clearly annoyed. "Thanks to the Witches."

"You don't like them much, do you?"

"We were doing just fine until the Chimera began to spread across the planet."

"When did this happen?"

"The Witches reopened the portals about twenty-five years ago. Though it seems like twenty thousand…"

I buried my hands deeper into my pockets and pulled at the loose threads in the corners. There was no love lost between the Druids and the Witches.

"Rory?"

He raised an eyebrow.

"What do I do with the cat?"

He laughed. "It does as it pleases. Delilah makes them as companions and guardians. Sometimes they pick their targets, other times they are happy to go where she takes them."

"I'm a target?"

"Not like that," he replied. "Whoever she put inside is aware enough to know you need its presence."

I frowned and tried to puzzle out the notion of a human soul in a cat and what it thought it could do for me. A fuzzy shoulder to cry on?

· · ·

"Who is it?"

"There's no way to tell."

An unknown human soul and another unsolved mystery.

"I didn't check, but I think it is a he, by the way," Rory added. "There were two wee balls back there."

I snorted, choking on my own spit. "Wee balls?"

Rory smirked. "What will you name him?"

"Sassenach," I drawled, causing him to laugh.

"Jaimie Fraser will be delighted, but technically, it *is* a bad name for an English person."

"Well, I don't know then. Maybe he'll tell me later."

We'd arrived at the apartments and I fished in my bag for the security fob Mrs. Campbell had given to me the day before.

The moment the tag beeped and I'd opened the door, Mrs. Campbell came charging out of her apartment like it was on fire.

"Elspeth! Oh, lass, where have you been?" she fussed. "I've been frightfully worried."

Rory mused his eyebrows. "Is this your landlady or your grandmother?"

She turned on him and glared. "And who might you be?"

I angled myself between them. "This is my friend—"

"Raurich," he interrupted, using his full name. "We've come to get Elspeth's belongings."

Mrs. Campbell scowled at him, then turned to me. "So you won't be staying then, lass?"

"I'm sorry," I told her. "It was unexpected, but I understand there'll be fees I'll have to pay."

"Yes," she said, clearly displeased at the sudden loss of income. "There will be a price. Only three days out of the month!" She clucked her tongue.

"We've got an appointment to keep," Rory said to me, conveying a cryptic message not to linger. "We best not miss it."

"I don't have much," I reassured him. "I'll be like, five minutes at most. Not even that."

"Right." He sat on the stairs and looked at Mrs. Campbell. "I'll wait here."

I hesitated, glancing at the older lady. Something else was happening here; something I wasn't seeing. Right then, I wished I understood how to work the Colour thing inside me.

Continuing up the stairs, I unlocked my apartment and turned on the light. Finding no gremlins or goblins hiding in the shadows, I strode into the bedroom and gathered my stuff, conscious that Owen might already be lurking outside.

I slipped my passport into my crossbody bag and zipped it closed. Then I packed the rest of my things into my suitcase. I hadn't taken much out, so once I'd stuffed my toiletries inside—along with a few dirty items of clothing—I was pretty much done.

I'd travelled light all my life, thanks to my dad. I was beginning to see it was a blessing to have a medium-sized suitcase with a third less stuff inside. But now I was beginning to understand who he was, and I wondered if it was a passive skill he'd been trying to teach me in case someone came searching for us—*like the Chimera.*

I shook my head and rolled the case out into the little living area. Looking at the half empty box of shortbread biscuits, I debated taking them with me. *Why not.* I smirked and shoved them into the top of my suitcase.

I heard a crash echo from downstairs as I zipped my case closed.

My heart leapt and I listened as muffled thudding and the sound of something shattering rattled the floor beneath my feet.

Rory.

I wrenched open the door and dragged my suitcase down the stairs, creating a deafening racket of my own.

Reaching the first-floor landing, I gasped when I saw Rory and Mrs. Campbell wrestling in the foyer… but it wasn't Mrs. Campbell anymore. The creature wore her clothes, but all traces of the stout old lady were gone.

In her place was a muscled, sinewy, grey humanoid monster with claws for fingers and razor-sharp teeth—I was now seeing the pointy pearly whites as a common trait with the Dark Fae.

Mrs. Campbell was trying to latch onto Rory's neck as he desperately stabbed his knife at her jugular. The pair tumbled over and Rory was on top, but he didn't have a clean shot as her claws erratically swiped at his face.

"*Rory!*" Acting on instinct, I picked up my suitcase, heaved it over my head, and threw it down the stairs.

He looked up just in time to roll out of the way. My suitcase hurtled through the air and collided with Mrs. Campbell, sending her into the opposite wall.

"Nice throw," Rory said, grinning up at me.

His knife flashed in his hand and he turned towards the creature. Blue shapes ignited around his arm and crawled over his hand while marks etched into the blade, flaring as they settled. *Were those runes?*

Mrs. Campbell pushed off the wall with a screech and leapt towards Rory, but he was ready for her. He stabbed upwards and the knife slammed into her chest, the blue light sparking as the blade cut her open from sternum to navel.

His Colour flared, protecting him as the Fae sailed over his head and its guts splattered everywhere. I covered my nose when a foul stench filled the foyer as her body landed with a thud .

"Oh my God," I whispered. "Oh. My. *God.*"

"Nope, not God," Rory said, wiping his knife on the creamy lace curtain covering the front door. "Fae trickery that is. Smells like a rotten fart, eh? Hey, your suitcase survived."

"But… Will…" I took a deep breath and

immediately regretted it. "The cops will be after us now." I'd never been in trouble before, not even in school. Zero detentions, right here. I'd never even gotten a speeding fine or parking ticket, and now here I was going for broke—murder in the first degree.

"The police are already after us, but not for this or anything on any official record. Fake Detective Owen will be along shortly to cover it up…and install a new Mrs. Campbell."

"A-a new Mrs. Campbell?" I backed away and tripped onto stairs, my arse coming to rest on the landing with a *plop*.

"Illusions," he told me. "Always look deeper, Elspeth."

Just when I thought things couldn't get any worse, my landlady turned out to be a Fae in disguise. Did she know who I was all this time? She had to be in on the conspiracy, helping Owen keep tabs on me. *The clueless Australian woman with no one to come looking for her.*

Rory knelt in front of me and picked up a strand of my hair. He peered at it for a moment, then smiled like he was only just beginning to understand something.

"Right now, we need to get you somewhere safe," he said, glancing at what was left of Mrs. Campbell. "Don't worry about all that, the Chimera will clean it up for us. We need to make ourselves scarce."

"What about the Druids? Are…? All this for a *suitcase*." My cheeks heated and I groaned.

"I guess I'm going to get grounded."

I shivered. "You say that like it happens a lot."

"Because it does." Rory smirked and rose to his feet. "Every day of the week and twice on Sundays." He held out his hand. "Are you coming? The Fae goop is starting to oxidise."

9

I sat on the end of Rory's bed, huddled in a blanket and stare at the fire.

The flames flickered as they burned the haphazard stack of logs in the hearth, popping and cracking as they were consumed.

Elspeth, what are you doing here?

Remembering the dream I had my first morning in Edinburgh, I realised it was a warning. My father was trying to contact me.

"Rory?"

"Yeah?" He looked up from my suitcase, the rag he'd been using to clean the last of the Fae goop from the hard outer shell dangling in his hand.

"Can Druids speak to spirits?"

His brow creased. "Some can, but that's a skill rarer than shapeshifting. We call them Spirit Walkers."

"What about the Fae?"

"Maybe." He shrugged and tossed the rag into the fire. "I don't really know."

The chances of me being able to Spirit Walk were slim, then. There went that idea.

Besides, it seemed like an advanced skill that could take years to master. The only time I'd used my so-called abilities was to stab Owen in the chest…and explode apparently. Luckily, I hadn't been conscious for that.

"What was Mrs. Campbell?" I asked, watching the flame turn green like it was burning a harsh chemical. "Was she a Chimera, too?"

"Your landlady was a Fae, but not a Chimera," he explained, sitting beside me. "She was a trickster. A lesser Dark Fae."

"A lesser Fae?"

"There are many different kinds of Fae, Elspeth. More than we'll ever know or encounter…not that I care to. The Chimera are more than enough." We watched the rag burn until the flame turned back to orange. "You want to talk to him, don't you?"

"It was worth asking. It's not every day you find out magic is real."

"You said your father was a hero?"

"He worked as an environmental scientist with the Australian government, but he was also a volunteer firefighter," I told him. "There were some serious bushfires across the country this past summer and… Well…" I swiped my hand across my eyes.

"Well then," Rory said. "You were right to be angry with me. I'm sorry."

I was beginning to understand why Dad had been so good at his job. He was a Druid and connected to the elements. He'd always known the best way to fight a fire or to preserve an area of natural heritage. My Dad was a supernatural environmentalist.

Rory shifted beside me. "Why did you come here, then?"

"Well, I kind of made a snap decision. I saw a poster in the window of a travel agent and..." I shrugged. "I felt drawn to it and before I knew it, I'd gotten on a plane."

"Ah," Rory said. "Without your father, your blood was calling you back to us."

I frowned and curled my lip. I didn't like the suggestion that I hadn't had a say in the matter.

"Don't look like that," he told me. "It's not attractive."

Without thinking, I punched him in the arm.

"*Ow*. Why was that for?"

"I don't believe in destiny," I said with a pout. "Destiny takes away choice."

"Well, one way or another, with supernatural creatures like us, blood will always win out."

"What do you mean?"

"The Druids are a community. We wander alone but are stronger together. Those tenants flow through our veins and bind us, Elspeth. With your father gone, you sought us out without even knowing it."

I lowered my gaze. "God, I wish he would have told me."

"I think he was trying to protect you."

"From the Chimera?"

"Maybe." Rory shrugged. "It's late. A mystery for another time, hey?" I went to stand, but he shook his head. "You can take my room tonight."

"I can't. I—"

"Don't fash yourself," he interrupted. "There's other places I can go. If you're here, I know you'll be safe." He pointed to the door. "I set runes into the wall so I'll know if something's not right."

I stared at the wall but saw nothing. "Runes?"

"Ach, you've got a lot to learn about our ways, Elspeth," he said with a laugh.

I grimaced and pulled the blanket tighter around my shoulders.

"There's a bathroom down the hall and a kitchen on the ground floor," he added. "Unless Jaimie has been here, there should be some food in the cupboards." He smiled and tapped his shoulder against mine. "He likes to eat. A lot."

"Uh, thanks."

He opened the door and peered out into the hall. "I'll come get you in the morning," he said. "Try and get some rest. The Elders will want to speak with you sooner or later."

"Elders?" I squeaked.

"Don't worry, they're not scary." He winked and closed the door behind him.

I collapsed onto the bed and studied the plaster ceiling as the sound of Rory's footsteps faded.

Elders, Druids, tricksters, fake Mrs. Campbell, runes… I couldn't keep up with all the twists and turns. It had only been three days, but I already couldn't recognise myself anymore.

What I did know was that I was now one of the hunted and had no way of protecting myself. The enemy was unknown. My past was unknown. And my powers were unknown. If I left now, I'd be toast.

For better or worse, I had to trust the Druids.

I just hoped they accepted me.

It took a few hours of tossing and turning, but eventually, I fell asleep.

When I woke the fire was out, but I'd received a visitor at some point. A warm ball of tabby-coloured fluff was curled in a tight ball beside me, its paw hooked over its nose to keep it warm.

I smiled and ran my hand along the cat's spine. Stirring, it stretched its paws out and rolled on its back, elongating its body.

Peering at me with emerald eyes, it purred.

"Hey, buddy," I murmured, running my hand through its soft belly fluff. "How did you get in?"

I shook my head as I watched the bluish-purple sparkles ripple through its tabby colouring. It was a construct made up of magic, it went where it pleased according to Rory.

"Well, if you're going to stick with me, I'll have to give you a name." I leaned over and grunted. "Yep, you're a boy all right. What do people call their cats anyway? Socks? Mittens?" The cat narrowed its eyes and rolled back onto its stomach. "Okay, something tough."

The cat yawned and flicked its tail back and forth. Entranced with the way his form rippled and glittered, I thought over some possible names. He was so cat-like, yet human at the same time.

"It's cold in here, isn't it?" I murmured, cupping his oversized face in my hand. "What I wouldn't do for a little fire in the fireplace right now."

"*Meow*," the cat declared.

"Fire, eh? What about Spark?" The cat seemed to shake his head. "Flame? Ember? Blaze? Inferno?" He seemed to like the last one but was still indifferent. "I don't know any Gaelic, but what about Latin? Ignis."

The cat meowed and butted its head against my face.

Rubbing my nose, I laughed. "Ignis it is, then."

With that settled, I found the bathroom and tinkered with the shower. I grimaced as the pipes rattled and groaned. Once the water had warmed, I scrubbed off what felt like a month's worth of uncertainty. Now I was ready to gather more.

Ignis was waiting for me when I returned to Rory's room.

The house was freezing cold and the radiators weren't on. I had no idea how to light a fire, so I huddled in my warmest jumper and wound my tartan scarf around my neck.

My stomach gurgled and I pressed my palm against my gut.

"I'm going to find the kitchen," I said to Ignis. "Are you coming? There might be something in there for you."

I left Rory's room and I made my way down the stairs. Ignis followed, his paws treading so silently, I almost forgot he was there.

The house was rather rickety and plain. Nothing hung on the walls but discoloured wallpaper which looked like it'd been stuck there in the seventeenth century—mint green with a pink rose pattern. It was peeling in the corners and had come apart at the seams—which was a fitting metaphor for my current life status.

The floorboards creaked as I made my way down the hall, the feeling I was trespassing tingled down my spine. The passageway angled a little to the right before opening into the kitchen, which had been painted fire-engine red, but that wasn't the first thing that caught my eye.

A woman sat at the table with her feet kicked up onto the chair next to her. She looked bored, like she was waiting for something…or someone. I glanced at the knife in her hand as she slid the tip underneath her fingernails, scraping out the gunk stuck underneath.

It looked like the one Rory carried, though a little longer and slimmer—less serrated hunting knife and more dagger-esque.

I could tell from the way she held herself that she was tall and athletic, not to mention confident and powerful. Her black hair hung long and straight, and her features gave her a feline appearance—an angular brow with almond-shaped eyes. To me, she felt predatory and my guard immediately went up.

Sensing my appearance, she lifted her head and stared at me with cool annoyance.

She glanced at Ignis, who prowled by my feet, and kicked her feet off the chair. "So, you're the one who almost killed Rory."

I opened my mouth, but my throat tightened, stopping me from replying. *I didn't almost kill anyone*, I wanted to say, but old tendencies had me shrinking away.

The woman sighed and rose to her feet. Walking towards me, I felt the air ripple around her—that was probably her Colour. She peered at me and picked up a strand of my hair.

Finally, I managed to move. "*Hey*." I jerked away.

The woman's expression didn't change. "Your hair is turning green."

"What?" I picked up a fistful of my auburn locks and found the ends were, in fact, turning an odd shade of mould. "What *is* that?"

"I think we know what your other half is," she said, her lip curling. She picked up the end of my scarf. "The Black Watch goes well on you."

Her thinly veiled insult barely registered and I blinked. "Other half?"

She smiled sweetly and fluttered her eyelashes, letting my scarf fall back into place. "Didn't Rory tell you?"

"At least he told me his name."

"Vanora," she stated. "And you are Elspeth." She said my name like she was spitting a bad taste out of her mouth. "What else could *it* be."

"Half what?" I asked again.

Vanora laughed. "You really are a clueless little mouse. Half Fae, *bò bhrònach*."

Half Fae? I stared at my hair, numb and unable to move.

"You've been here all of five minutes and already you've put Rory in danger no less than three times and almost killed him once."

"I-I didn't ask for his help, he—"

"He may have appointed himself as your *neach-gleidhidh*, but he is promised to *me*," she snarled. "Don't forget that."

There was movement behind me and her expression turned sweet. Swatting me out of the way, she slunk across the kitchen to where Rory stood in the doorway.

"Rory," she purred. "I'm glad to see you doing so well after what had happened yesterday."

"Thanks," he said, glancing at me.

"No doubt the Elders will want to see you both," she added. "I have duties of my own to attend to." She looked at me, her expression darkening. "I'll see you later."

She sauntered down the hall and out the front door. It slammed a moment later, making the whole house shudder—a feat considering it was built out of stone.

Rory glanced after Vanora and from the look on his face, I knew he could see through her theatrics.

"What's her problem?" I asked with a scowl.

"It's complicated."

"Like everything else around here."

Rory sighed. "There are those amongst us who believe we aren't worthy of reaching the homeland. Vanora is one of them. I fear it's turned her heart hard."

I shook my head. "Why wouldn't you be worthy?"

"Those who don't make it through the Darklands are deemed unworthy and taken by the guardians of that place. They become shadows, doomed to wander the darkness forever." He grimaced. "Our people never made it."

Ignis leapt onto the table and let out a loud *meow*.

"Oh, I see you've found your way back to the food again," he said to him. "Did you give him a name yet?"

"Ignis."

"Ignis?" He scratched the construct on the head. "Latin for fire. Cool."

I shrugged. "It seemed like he wanted a name that started with 'I' and I was cold."

"*Priorities*." Rory turned to the fridge. "Have you eaten yet? We've got milk." He opened the door and immediately closed it with a disappointed grimace. "Maybe not."

"I don't feel hungry anymore," I told him, thinking about what Vanora had said. *Half Fae.* "Rory?"

He raised an eyebrow.

"What does *bò bhrònach* mean?" I stumbled over the unfamiliar language, my cheeks heating.

"Don't worry about Vanora," he said, inadvertently revealing it was an insult…and not a pleasant one. "Us Druids are a tight knit lot. There aren't that many of us, so your appearance has caused quite the stir. There's talk of prophecy and mutations and all kinds of nonsense."

"Mutations?"

"Old wives' tales," he said with a wave of his hand. "I wouldn't believe anything you hear."

I lifted up a handful of hair. "What about green hair suddenly meaning that I'm half Fae?"

Rory shuffled nervously. "Uh, I didn't think it was my place to say anything. The Elders wanted to speak to you first."

"So, it's a thing that everybody knows except for me?" I let out a cry of frustration.

It felt like high school all over again. *Make yourself small, Elspeth, so no one notices you. Don't excel, it'll only make you a target. If they can't see you, they won't bully you.* Too bad it made me almost fail all my final exams, so all I could apply for at university was a useless Arts degree. I needed an overall mark of eighty-five to scrape in the bottom of the Bachelor of Science intake, but the number I managed didn't bear mentioning.

"Take a deep breath," Rory urged. "You'll get some answers from the Elders."

"They want to see me? Now?"

He nodded and patted Ignis again. "C'mon. It's time to show you where we really live."

10

———

Rory led me to the basement of the house.

He clicked on the light and a dusty bulb illuminated the cold, damp room. I shivered and rubbed my hands up and down my arms, more confused than cold.

There was nothing down here except for the old boiler, a few broken chairs, and a trapdoor set into the floor. And spiderwebs, lots of spiderwebs.

"Is this the part where you murder me and cut me up into little pieces?" I asked. "Because I don't get it."

Rory laughed. "No, it's not nearly as dramatic as that."

I glanced at the trapdoor. "You're not going to make me go down there, are you?"

"Ach," he muttered and pressed his hand against the wall.

My breath caught as the stone began to ripple. Splotches of black appeared and began to spread across the surface, glistening with colour that reminded me of a rainbow on top of an oil slick. Finally, it formed the shape of an arched door.

"It's a portal," Rory said.

That was the ability the Chimera were so desperate to get their hands on? I stared at the surface, but I couldn't see what was on the other side.

"You won't see much through this one," Rory added. "There's a tunnel on the other side, then another portal."

"An extra layer of security?" I wondered.

"Aye."

"Will it hurt?"

He smiled and shook his head. "Ach, no. It feels like splashing cool water on your face."

Shrugging, I stepped through the portal and emerged in a dark tunnel.

On the other side, I shivered as coldness trickled down my spine. It felt like walking through a wall of water without actually getting wet.

Rory appeared behind me in the darkness and scooted past, taking the lead. He led me down the passage, the sound of our footsteps echoed off the hard bedrock. I kept close, afraid I'd be left behind in the dark.

There was nothing remarkable about the tunnel— it smelled like damp earth and mould.

"The Druids you will see here are descendants from five families that became lost in the Darklands,"

Rory explained. "Elinian, Maerinn, Cuihan, Ariennir, and Odhweine."

"Which one are you?"

"Maerinn. Mackenzie is my stage name."

"How many Druids are there?" I asked. "Or is it still a secret?"

"You'll see…"

He stopped suddenly and I smacked into his back.

"Ow," I grumbled. "A little warning, please."

"Past this door lies the Warren," he said. "It's a series of tunnels and houses carved underneath Edinburgh, folded inside an illusion."

"An illusion?"

"Technically, it's a pocket of reality that's been separated from the Earth."

I rolled my eyes. "Oh, now that you mention it…"

Rory laughed and opened the door. Muted light spilled into the tunnel as another portal rippled into life.

We stepped into another passage, but this one was nothing like the last. Volcanic glass and gemstones made up the walls—shining obsidian swirled with dappled turquoise—and sconces with jagged globes were placed at regular intervals, lighting the pathway. For an underground warren, it was rather bright in here.

"They're crystals," I said, gazing at the pointed clusters in the sconces. "Glowing crystals."

"Aye," Rory replied. "Quartz. They hold simple prisms rather well."

"Like batteries?"

"Yes." He nodded, poking the nearest sconce with his finger and the crystal brightened slightly. "They still need to be charged every now and then."

"But how do they work?" Science had gone completely out of the window, but I thought I'd read someplace that quartz was good at conducting energy, but was it metaphoric spiritual vibes or tangible electricity?

"Forget about the light globes," Rory said with a chuckle. "Those are nothing." He grasped my shoulder and turned me around. *"Look at this."*

It was then that I realised we stood on a large balcony which overlooked an enormous cavern. Above, points of light sparkled on the ceiling, but it was the towering willow tree in the centre that had me doing a double-take.

I clutched the stone edge of the balcony and gaped. Not only was it the largest willow I'd ever seen, but a great deal of the weeping frond also hovered towards the roof of the cavern. It reminded me of an underwater sea creature floating in a crystal ocean—the light down here was blue-tinted, but dim.

"The willow symbolises the connection between the earth and sky," Rory told me. "Mostly between the water and the moon, but down here it's more literal."

"But… How does it grow?"

"Magic," he whispered. Rory chuckled and

threaded his arm though mine. "*Salle* is the centre of the Warren."

"*Salle*?"

"The Druidic word for willow."

My gaze travelled downward, taking in the view below. The floor of the cavern was an underground garden with stone paths, grass, and what looked like flowers. The shadow of multiple tunnels opened in the walls and other balconies appeared all over the walls. There must be a dozen levels at least, and who knew how far those passages led?

"It's a whole city," I whispered.

"Not quite," Rory told me. "But it's large enough. You're looking at eight hundred years of construction."

"You've lived here the whole time?"

"Not all of it, but close." He gestured for me to follow. "C'mon. They'll be waiting for us in the library."

I walked through the Warren in a state of shock. There were dozens of passages and rooms leading farther into the volcanic rock. Crystals had been imbedded in almost every surface and runes were carved into lintels and doorways. Wooden boards hung over some entrances, acting as signposts pointing out passages that lead to things like a herbalist, the kitchen, market, gardens, and houses.

Speaking of gardens, here and there, plants had taken root in the rock, growing vines along passage walls and clumps of flowers bloomed underneath glowing sconces, their coloured petals stretching towards the light.

We emerged into the cavern we'd seen from above and stood before a set of large, round, wooden doors set into the rock. Oblivious to the Druids staring at us, I began to get the shakes. It felt like I'd stepped inside a sacred temple and I was the out-of-place non-believer. Vanora's snide Fae comment didn't help the situation, either.

Rory rapped twice on the door, then opened it.

The room was large and round, the walls clad with stained wood panels and inset with tall bookshelves overflowing with leather-bound tomes. The floor was carpeted with a thick emerald green pile which looked like springy moss, and desks and various seated areas littered the open space, separated by glass display cases full of delicate artefacts I was desperate to look at.

There were more crystal sconces, though they glowed with a warm hue, giving the library a warm, homely feel.

Looking up, my breath caught as I saw the entire ceiling was made of crystal. A massive amethyst geode dome shimmered in the light, hundreds of thousands of points aiming down at the library. I could feel the Colour radiating off it—or at least, that's what I thought it was—and I was more drawn to it the closer I looked.

"Beautiful, isn't it?" a female voice asked.

My heart leapt and my gaze locked on a pair of

iridescent blue irises. The woman before us was petite, but her presence was overwhelming. Silver strands threaded through her black locks, and the lines around her eyes gave me a glimpse at her true age, though she seemed timeless.

I was half expecting for her to wear flowing robes like a pagan priestess, but she looked more like a bohemian art teacher. She wore black jeans with a loose-fitting cream- and blue-patterned shirt and a matching long blue crocheted vest over the top. Multiple necklaces with crystal points and silver charms jangled as she reached out her hands in greeting.

Delicate lines of light marked her exposed arms and I realised they were runes. I wondered what they were for.

Rory nudged me forwards. "Elspeth, this is Delilah Odhweine, Elder of the Darkland Druids."

This was Delilah? I stared at her in awe instead of the ceiling.

She laughed and took my hands in hers, her welcome a lot warmer than Vanora's had been.

"Elspeth, welcome to the Warren."

"Uh, I… Thank you," I managed to reply.

"I see my latest creation has taken a liking to you," she said with a chuckle.

Ignis meowed and strolled across the library, where he leapt into an empty space in one of the bookshelves and curled up and went to sleep. The cat was so stealthy, I had forgotten he was here.

"She named him Ignis," Rory said.

"Ignis?" Her gaze searched mine. "Interesting."

"It uh… It just came to me and he seemed to like it," I said lamely.

"We hear you've had quite the adventure," Delilah said to me. "It all must be confusing to say the least."

I nodded. "You can say that again."

"Come, let me introduce you to the other Elders." She lifted her hand and shooed Rory away, her silver rings glinting in the crystal light. "We have much to talk about."

Delilah led me through the library to where a man and a woman sat at a large oak table.

Gesturing to the man, she said, "This is Shor Elinian."

He nodded once, his impassive gaze never leaving me. Even though he was seated, I could tell he was tall and proud from the way he held his shoulders. He had short-cropped greying hair and wore a simple black collared shirt with the top button undone.

"And here is Rowen Ariennir," Delilah added.

Rowen was much like Delilah with her grace and poise, though her hair was a brilliant burnt orange colour with threads of iridescent silver. Her gaze was equally as unreadable, and my nerves began to reach an uncomfortable level in my bowels.

Delilah urged me to take a seat at the table, then took her place beside the other Elders. Suddenly, I felt like I was on a job interview and they were about to ask what I thought constituted as good customer service.

Shor was the first to speak. "Rory explained to us that you didn't know about your heritage."

I looked between them, wondering if I was on trial. "I had no idea… If I had, then I wouldn't have put Rory in danger like that. I—"

"Hush, child," Rowen said. "We don't blame you for your near miss with the Chimera. We can't judge those who act without knowledge fairly."

I blinked. *Did she just call me stupid?*

"The other Druids said some things," I began. "That I'm half something else…"

"It's true," Shor said. "You are half Fae. Now that we see you, the threads are clear within your Colours."

I looked to Delilah, my eyes widening. Were they saying I was the enemy here? Were they going to kick me out and make me fend for myself?

"Don't worry, Elspeth," she said. "We won't seek to turn you away."

"It's clear your Druid blood dominates your Fae," Rowen mused. "Rory said it was your Colour that saved you both from the Chimera."

I nodded.

"You were lucky," Shor stated. "It could have ended badly."

The explosion was already dangerous if I took Rory's account as face value. 'Going supernova' seemed pretty serious.

"Why didn't I know what I was before now?" I asked. "If I was born with this, wouldn't I have been able to do things?"

Delilah smiled. "Your abilities were blocked, likely in order to hide you from the Chimera."

"And us," Shor declared.

"But, I…" I took a deep breath. "Why would my father hide me?"

"A child who is both Druid and Fae comes with many unknowns. If you aligned with the Chimera, they could use your abilities for their own ends. If you aligned with us…"

I snorted and curled my lip. "You could use me as a weapon against the Chimera."

"There is no doubt that it is a dangerous precedent being sent here," Rowen noted. "One we haven't foreseen."

So, half Fae Druids weren't common. If I was to believe the troubled expressions on the Elders' faces, it was likely I was the first and only who had ever existed.

"How about letting me make up my own mind?" I declared. "Maybe I don't want to be a weapon? Maybe I just want to be a normal woman."

"The Chimera have caused us a great deal of harm, Elspeth," Rowan explained. "The distinction between Light and Dark is not as simple as it seems."
It never was.

"Then who was my father?" I looked between the

Elders. If they were the oldest and wisest of the Druids, then they had to know. "Who was he *really*?"

"Your father…" Delilah began. "He was a Druid and his loss…his *final* loss, will be mourned greatly."

My heart leapt. "Did you know him?"

"It's a long tale, child," Rowen said.

"And my mother?"

The Elders fell silent and I knew they didn't know anything about her—anything they were willing to admit anyway.

Why were they stonewalling me? Maybe they didn't trust me yet. Apparently, my allegiance could go either way and I could go full Fae apocalypse on them.

I stilled. Was that it? Was it more than just having Fae blood?

"We don't have to settle on a final outcome here and now," Delilah said, rising. "All this talk about war and danger has unsettled the welcome you deserve, Elspeth. You carry the blood of your father and thus, are embraced by the Druids."

I stared up at her, confused as hell. "I am?"

"It is already settled," she replied. "You shall stay with us for the time being and learn how to control your Colour. Perhaps more answers surrounding your Fae heritage will manifest and then we shall all understand a little clearer."

"What if I want to go home?" I asked.

Delilah frowned. "Returning to the surface now

would only put you in danger. I fear the Chimera still search the city. They are ruthless creatures."

"So, I'm stuck here?"

"Not stuck," she murmured. "Just…waylaid." She clapped her hands and grinned at me. "Shall we walk, Elspeth?"

It must have been her signal that the hearing was over because Shor huffed, clearly put out that he couldn't question me further. Rowen was harder to read but nodded her acceptance. Delilah must have some serious clout around these parts.

The Elders seemed to disappear into thin air, and I looked around, stunned. Delilah rose and wandered through the library as if nothing had happened. I had to jog to catch up, almost falling out of my chair in the process.

"All the items you see in the cases were brought with us through the Darklands," she explained. "The books came after…once we began to build the Warren."

I peered into display cases, studying the items within—blades, crystals, and even clothing—and tried to scan spines of books as we passed.

"You must have other questions," she added. "You may ask me some, if you wish."

I sighed, knowing the answers I really wanted wouldn't be forthcoming. Simple it was, then.

"Are all Fae bad?" I wondered.

"Not all are Dark," Delilah explained. "There are two sides to every coin, and so it is with the Fae."

"So not all of them want to kill you?"

She smiled and placed her hand on my shoulder. "*Us*."

I drew in a shaky breath.

"You may be different, but you are one of us."

"So my Fae half might not be Chimera?"

Delilah nodded. "*Exactly*. Things are not as dire as they seem, no?"

"I guess not." I paused by a display case and studied the ornate silver knives within. Crystal points were set in the end of the handles, while runes had been carved along the length of the blades. "But what if I turn out to be one of the bad kind?"

The Druid placed her hand on my shoulder and smiled. "But what if you aren't? There's no way of knowing until we know, so worrying is only going to force your heart away from more pressing matters."

I blinked, dazed at her philosophical way of explaining things. "Which are?"

"Embracing your birthright." She laughed and we strolled towards the door. "Raurich has volunteered to be your *neach-gleidhidh*."

"What is that exactly?" I asked.

"It's Gaelic. In English it means a few things, but we use it as guardian." She chuckled and shook her head. "Our language is a strange thing. We tend to adopt words from all the places we've been and twist them to suit our needs."

"Rory said something to me in Irish Gaelic, but

I'm afraid I never learned the Scottish, either. My dad, he…" He never spoke anything but English.

Delilah nodded. "I understand. Perhaps Raurich will teach you, though he takes a less scholarly approach to Druidism. Ah, here we are."

We'd arrived at the library doors and she opened them, letting in a cool breeze from the cavern beyond.

"Go," she said, gently nudging me forwards. "The Warren is yours to explore."

Druids were milling about in the cavern, and as we stood there, we drew curious glances that made my shyness flare. Some were friendly, but some reminded me of the welcome Vanora had given me. Prejudice simmered under the surface and I was beginning to realise that this world wasn't quite as magical as it first seemed.

Why did I have the feeling I'd just been taken in by the lesser evil? Perhaps it was like Rory had said about the Druids when they first came to Earth. I'd fallen into a new world, only to find myself in the middle of a war I didn't understand. Now it seemed like my existence was an unexpected boon that could tip the balance. I would become a pawn, but only if I let them.

Maybe learning how to use my Colours was the only way I could take charge of my destiny. If I understood how to fight back, maybe I would win this time.

Well, there was only one way to find out.

I took a deep breath and stepped into the Warren.

11

———————

I stood in the cavern, looking up at the tree and the artificial crystal sunlight. It really was something to see.

Birds played amongst the branches, chirping and carrying on. From the way their wings shimmered, I knew they were more of Delilah's constructs.

Looking around, I realised Ignis hadn't followed me from the library and for a moment, I considered going back for him, but then I remembered what Rory had said the day before. Constructs came and went as they pleased. When Ignis was ready, he'd find me.

A few Druids sat amongst the twist of roots underneath the canopy, reading and talking amongst themselves. Every now and then they'd glance my way or a passerby would do a double-take, but no one spoke to me and I lacked the courage to take the initiative.

I stood awkwardly, fighting off the embarrassment that threatened to flood my cheeks. I wasn't sure what to do with myself. Craning my neck, I couldn't see Rory anywhere. *Awkward.*

It's time to stop being a scared girl and be a badarse woman, I thought, heaving a sigh. *Be like Dad.*

Seeing the sign for the kitchen, I decided I was hungry after all. Holding my head high, I strode through the cavern and down the tunnel. *Confidence, Elspeth.* But when I stepped into the kitchen, I began to tremble.

It was bustling with activity. Druids sat around stone tables, laughing and talking amongst themselves. At the far end was the actual kitchen, where a spread of delicious smelling food had been laid out in an elaborate banquet.

I tentatively walked the length of the room, feeling the weight of dozens of eyes burning into my flesh. I stood before the food and my stomach rumbled. There were piles of freshly baked rolls, a pot of stew, salads, rice, cakes, and other assorted dishes. A pile of bowls, plates, and cutlery sat at one end, but I wasn't sure I was allowed to take any.

A woman walked by, and when she saw my hesitation, she turned. Like many of the other Druids I'd seen, she was lithe and pretty, but instead of long flowing hair, hers was cropped in a cute pixie cut. She had some of the same blueish runes tattooed on her arms, too.

"Are you all right?" she asked.

"I don't know…" I looked at the food longingly.

"Ah, Rory left you out on your arse, did he?" she asked. "Typical. That man flits in and out like a dragonfly who thinks he owns the world." I took her long-winded sentence to mean she thought Rory was arrogant.

"I'm sorry, who are you?"

"Oh, I'm Darby," she said. "Nice to meet you."

"I'm—"

"Elspeth, I know. Help yourself," she added. "You don't need to do anything special. Everyone is taken care of here."

"Darby, what are you doing?" Another woman appeared beside her and tugged on her arm, giving me a wary glance.

"Oh, I…" She gave me an apologetic smile and allowed her friend to pull her away.

Sighing, I took a tray and filled a bowl with thick, hearty stew. When I was done, I kept my head down and moved through the room, conscious that no matter what I did, I would still be the centre of attention.

I stood in the middle of the kitchen holding my tray, feeling like the nerd in the high school cafeteria. Looking around, all the tables were taken and every open seat abruptly became taken.

Sighing, for what felt like the millionth time, I took the bowl and spoon and dumped the tray, deciding to go back to the willow tree and wait for Rory or Ignis to find me.

As I was about to leave, I spotted a familiar face shovelling food into his mouth at an alarming pace. He looked different clothed and I snorted, remembering how Rory made fun of his 'wee willy'.

I paused by the table. "Jaimie Fraser?"

"Ach, just Jaimie," he replied, looking up at me. "Rory was just playing with you, lass."

"Oh, I'm sorry."

"Don't fash." He waved a hand at me. "You got a place to sit? Park your arse there, lass."

I shrank slightly. "You don't mind?"

"Ach, not at all." He resumed eating with all the decorum of his German Shepard shape.

I slid onto the stone bench and set my bowl before me and poked at my stew.

"So, you met the Elders, eh?" Jaimie asked. "They're our own little triskele. Shor is the most like fire. Rowen is the earth and Delilah is the air. Or at least, I think that's how it goes."

Movement beside me pulled my gaze and I saw Vanora circle the table. She stood behind Jaimie and placed her hands on his broad shoulders as if she was laying claim to him.

"Be careful, Jaimie," she said, glaring at me. "We don't know what that mouldy hair is capable of yet."

My hand tightened around my spoon.

Jaimie shrugged her off. "Leave off, Vanora."

"Just saying," she purred before she flicked her hair over her shoulder and sauntered away.

I narrowed my eyes at her receding back and

grimaced. It didn't take long for the resident bully to make herself known.

Jaimie rolled his eyes. "Vanora's got claws. Watch her, lass."

"Oh, I've already had the pleasure." I gave her one last glance. "What's her deal? She said she and Rory…"

He shrugged. "Kind of."

"Kind of?"

"Druids are few and far between," he replied. "There's a small gene pool, if you know what I'm saying."

"No, I—" Suddenly, I understood what he was getting at. Rory and Vanora were betrothed in order to ensure the Druids ongoing survival. "Oh. Never mind."

It wasn't just distrust over my apparent Fae heritage I faced. They wouldn't want my polluted genes muddying up the waters, let alone give me a place in their precious homeland. This place was turning out to be less and less magical than it had seemed at first and more and more like a regular human snake pit.

I'd come to Scotland looking for answers and understanding…and meaning. A place to belong. Community. Acceptance.

It was already jarringly clear I wasn't going to find much of that here.

"Don't worry, lass," Jaimie said. "He won't

abandon you because of Vanora. He'll still be your *neach-gleidhidh*. The Elders have decreed it."

"It's not that," I managed to get out.

Jaimie snorted and his eyes widened. "You're into—"

"It's not that, either," I snapped.

"Stop antagonising her," Rory declared, materialising out of thin air. He sat beside me and stole a slice carrot out of my bowl. "I found you a place to stay."

"Didn't anyone ever tell you it was rude to stick your fingers into someone else's food?" I grumbled.

He held up his hands in defence. "Hey, watch it. The Elders give you a grilling or something?"

"I told her about the gene pool," Jaimie declared.

"Ach, *dùin do ghob*," Rory fired back.

"You want this?" I asked, sliding the bowl towards Jaimie. "I'm not very hungry."

"You've hardly had anything to eat since our adventure on Calton Hill," Rory declared.

"Is that what you call almost dying? An *adventure*?"

"You two are going to get along just fine." Jaimie chuckled and slid the bowl towards him with a sly wink.

"Like I was saying," Rory stated, "I found you a place to stay."

"Would you like to show it to me?" I asked.

"Watch yourself, lad," Jaimie said, digging into what was left of my lunch. "She looks sweet, but under that façade is a fierce Druidess."

I knew he was only playing around, but I wasn't in the mood. My magical awakening was rapidly turning into a nightmare.

"C'mon," Rory said, "let's get out of here."

"He eats a lot," I noted as we left the kitchen.

"Shapeshifters use a lot of energy," Rory explained.

"Is that why he's muscly?"

"No, but it helps considering what he likes to change into."

I wondered what other animals Jaimie could shapeshift into while Rory led me through a tunnel deeper into the Warren. There were two dogs that day on Calton Hill—the German Shepard and the scrappy little mutt. Maybe he'd been both all along.

"Here we are." We stopped outside a door in a quiet area of the caves. I looked down the tunnel, noting the other entrances staggered along the length. It must be a residential area.

Rory opened the door and gestured for me to go first.

Inside, the walls were more turquoise, though little shards of obsidian and quartz shimmered amongst the stone like fancy terrazzo. A double bed was pushed to the left—with a colourful purple, blue, and green blanket over the top—and a dresser sat against the right wall. Two doors flanked the far-right corner leading to places unknown, and a woven jute mat covered most of the stone floor. To finish off the look, a quartz crystal light was fixed into the ceiling and a landscape painting hung on the wall behind us.

It was beautiful, but they could have put me in a broom closet and I would have thought the same thing.

"If you want the light on, you wave you hand over this rune." Rory showed me, and the crystal light dimmed and brightened. "When you learn your Colours, you'll be able to do it without getting out of bed." He wigged his eyebrows. "Handy on those cold Scottish mornings. Cool, huh?"

"It's not what I was expecting…"

He frowned. "You don't like it?"

"No, *I love it.*"

My answer seemed to please him. "Just wait until you see the bathroom."

"There's a bathroom?"

Rory opened one of the doors, revealing a closet. "Nope. Not that one." He turned the knob on the second and edged it open. "Ah, this is it."

I followed him into the little en suite and was once again taken by surprise.

There was a mirror and basin, and a porcelain toilet that had been plumbed into a network of mysterious pipes. The walls and floors were the same as the bedroom—turquoise—but someone had the foresight to put a fuzzy grey mat on the floor.

I inspected the shower and the confusingly modern fixtures behind the curtain. We were in a magical cave folded into a pocket of space time, so how was there modern plumbing?

"Where does the water go?" I asked.

"Recycled, I suppose. Don't ask about the toilet. Doesn't bear mentioning."

I edged back into the bedroom and studied the painting. It looked like the landscape of the world above, before Edinburgh sprouted up into a densely packed city. There was the Medieval castle on the hill and the rise leading up to it.

"I went back and got your things while you were in the library," Rory said, pointing to my suitcase which sat at the foot of the bed. "That's why I was late getting back. You don't have a lot of stuff."

"I'm a minimalist."

He chuckled. "Then you've come to the right place. Druids love travelling light."

A wave of emotion welled in my chest as I looked around the room. He'd done all this for me.

I turned away, pretending to admire the room as I gathered my wits. So far, he and Jaimie were the only Druids who'd welcomed me. Delilah had too, but she also came with a hidden agenda. Rory was just nice because… Well, because he *was* nice.

"Do you have a room like this, too?" I managed to ask.

"Not really. I'm in the city a lot, so I just sleep upstairs."

My emotions back in check, I turned. "What do you do up there exactly?

"Patrol, spy, protect the entrances to the Warren. Live life on the edge."

"If the Chimera are hunting you, wouldn't it be safer down here?"

"Perhaps," he mused. "But why should we let them take the Earth from us? We're just as entitled to walk it as any other creature. They won't scare us away, Elspeth. If we can fight back, then we have a chance."

"Makes sense." Twenty-five years was a long time to live underground without seeing the actual sun.

"So what did the Elders say?" I could tell he'd been itching to ask since the moment we were alone.

I scowled. "They said a lot, but hardly any of it had substance."

Rory laughed and shook his head. "The Elders can be a little…vague," he explained. "Us younger generations are more direct. It comes from living amongst humans, I think." As close as their mystical fairytale city could get them to Edinburgh, it was a little ironic.

"They wouldn't tell me who my father was," I said. "They blatantly told me it was a story for another time. Why would they keep it from me?"

"The Elders always have a reason for doing what they do."

"Even if you believe it's wrong?"

He seemed surprised that I'd question their logic. "They've never led us astray."

"You perhaps," I muttered, deciding to keep the

other revelation to myself. The one where I could be manipulated into being a weapon against the Chimera—and vice versa. It was likely that Rory already knew, but I didn't want to talk about it, not after the hostility I'd felt out in the Warren.

I got fighting back, but wouldn't it just be better if the Druids could find their way home? Go back to the Darklands and fight for their true world? That's what they wanted; it had been eight hundred years. What was stopping them?

"That's a serious frown," Rory stated. "What's weighing your brow down?"

"Have you ever been to the Darklands?"

"I haven't had that honour," he replied.

"Has anyone? I mean, have they tried to go back and find a way to your homeland?"

"Not since we first came here, no." He shrugged. "There are only a few left who remember it."

I paused. "Wait…"

"Delilah was one of the few who first made our home here," Rory told me. "And Rowen, too."

"That would make her…" I didn't want to say it out loud, but Rory did it for me.

"Around nine hundred, but don't mention it around her, especially not Rowen."

"How long do Druids live?"

"Depends."

I scowled. "On?"

"Lifestyle choices."

"How old are you?"

Rory winked and pressed his finger to his lips. "I'll never tell."

"*Wait.*" My heart skipped a beat. "How long will I live?"

"Don't know. You're new."

I was more confused the deeper down the rabbit hole I went. I snorted and shook my head. Alice in Wonderland, indeed.

"Delilah doesn't seem like someone who wouldn't be worthy," I stated, picking up my earlier tangent. "Is that why no one has been back?"

Rory shrugged and turned away, plucking at a leaf on the vine hanging over the bed. Okay, so that was a point of contention. Some Druids seemed to think returning to their home was impossible, while others still had hope.

"Maybe because you haven't been there, you're still—"

"We'll begin training tomorrow," he said. "Okay?"

My shoulders sank and I nodded. "Whatever you say, *neach-gleidhidh*. Did I say that right?"

His lips quirked, softening the air between us a little. "No, but we'll work on that, too." He nodded at my suitcase. "You better get settled. I'll come find you in the morning."

"What if I get lost?"

"It's impossible to get lost in the Warren," he told me. "All paths eventually lead back to *Salle*. The willow."

I nodded and he opened the door.

"Rory?"

He turned.

"Am I doing the right thing?" I asked.

He shrugged. "Right now, it's the only thing."

I didn't know what to say, so I offered him a half-smile. There probably wasn't anything I could have said anyway.

Once he was gone, I opened all the drawers in the dresser and explored the nooks and crannies in my room. It was the same thing I did whenever I checked into a hotel, but this time there were no complimentary toiletries or Bible in the bedside table.

In the bathroom, I splashed water on my face, thinking about everything the Elders had said. They didn't know my mother, but my father… Why had the Chimera murdered him? Was it because of me? The more I thought about it, the more I realised it probably was. I was half-Fae—and if the fear I faced from the other Druids was to be believed, I likely held the powers of one—and as a Druid, I also had the ability to open portals. Blood called to blood and they believed I would be torn between sides. Was that it?

I was beginning to worry it was something more sinister than the Chimera. Was he trying to protect me from *both* sides?

I cursed and dragged my fingers through my hair. Catching my reflection, I noticed the green had spread. At least it was a nice shade of glowing emerald and not some putrid khaki.

It didn't matter. It still marked me as different. *Dangerous*.

I stared into the mirror, studying the freckles across my nose, and trying to find the similarities that marked me as my father's daughter.

If I concentrated hard enough, I could almost see Dad standing behind me. I placed my hand on the mirror and choked back a sob. I needed him now more than ever, but he was gone. If only I was one of those mysterious Spirit Walkers, then maybe I could go into death and bring him back.

But I wasn't. I didn't know what I was.

And that was the problem.

12

By the following morning, two things had happened.

Ignis had materialised inside my room and proceeded to hog the entire bed…and the green had taken over more of my hair.

I was scowling at a problematic clump in the mirror when a knock pulled me away from my pouting. My mobile phone had lost its charge days ago and to be totally honest, I'd forgotten all about checking my email—not that I got any. Point was, I had no idea what time it was.

Opening the door, I found Rory on the other side.

"Catch," he declared, tossing something at me.

I fumbled the apple he'd thrown at me and almost dropped it onto the floor.

"Watch it," I warned.

"You look comfortable."

I looked down at my leggings, slouchy army-green

jumper—that covered my backside *and* frontside—combat boots, and woolly speckled grey socks that poked out the tops. I topped it off with a shrug. "I didn't know what training entailed."

It mustn't be much because Rory was wearing his usual getup—T-shirt, jeans, and his own stompy black boots. I did note that he'd managed to comb his hair, which seemed too much effort for most men. Suddenly, I wondered how old he really was.

"That'll do," he said. "C'mon." He paused and looked over my shoulder. "Is the flea bag coming?"

"Don't call him a flea bag," I scolded. "Ignis?" The cat lifted his head and his tail flicked, but there was no other movement. "Trust me to get the lazy construct."

"Newbies are flaky," Rory told me as I closed the door behind me. "They like to sleep a lot. Delilah says its because fractured souls take time to adjust to their new realities. How was the shower, by the way?"

"Quite nice actually. The Warren has excellent water pressure."

He chuckled as we walked through the tunnels. I noticed we were in a section I hadn't seen yet and wondered where this mysterious training was taking place.

We passed underneath an arch, then through another door, emerging into a large, open room.

Mirrors lined one turquoise quartz wall, though the others were bare besides the Druid's trademark crystal lighting system. A pile of mats and pillows had been piled in one corner and a door led to another room beyond, though there were no clues as to what was inside.

"What is this place?" I wondered out loud.

"It's used for training," Rory replied. "Everything from Colour to combat skills. That's why the floor is squishy."

I frowned. "Combat skills?"

"We're no elite warriors, but we have to protect ourselves somehow."

"Makes sense."

I caught my reflection in one of the mirrors and frowned. In more direct light, my hair was taking on a life of its own. Soon, my natural auburn locks would be no more.

"Great," I muttered, drawing Rory's attention.

He stood beside me and peered at my reflection. "What?"

"My hair. I know people want to be special, but not *different*. I may as well have a neon sign over my head that says 'Fae' with an arrow pointing downward."

"Don't worry about what other people think," he said. "It doesn't matter. I like green—it's the most important colour in nature besides brown."

"Brown?" I rolled my eyes. "Who likes brown?"

"No one's keeping score."

Score. It made me think of the day before, when I was mulling over my human high school experience.

"Tell that to the arsehole who graded my exams," I muttered.

Rory tilted his head to the side, confused.

"Never mind."

"I will mind because it's blocking your Colours."

I screwed up my nose. "Huh?"

"Emotional blockages," he prodded. "It's a thing, remember?"

I heaved a sigh and rolled my shoulders. "I was a complete reject growing up. I was picked on, bullied, squashed down… I learned to make myself small and quiet to avoid being a target. No one would notice me if I didn't excel, and I'd be safe. All it did was make me stupid. I could have gone on to study Earth sciences and be like my dad, but I got nowhere near the score I needed to get into a Bachelor of Science degree. I was so far away, my dreams may as well have been in another galaxy."

"You're not stupid, Elspeth. It's just a score."

"That stopped me from having a future where I could do something great," I cried. "Do you realise how useless an Arts degree is when it comes time to get a job? I do! I hate them and I hate—" I clamped my mouth shut and fought back a sudden onslaught of tears.

"Yourself?" Rory asked.

My jaw tensed, but I didn't grace him with a reply. The truth hurt too much. I was stupid for thinking they were the ones who'd stopped me from having the future I wanted. The only person who'd screwed up was me. I was weak, plain and simple.

"Bottling up your emotions won't do you any good," he said. "What happened in that close with Owen was a warning. If you hold onto too much—"

"I'll explode. *Literally*." I scoffed, "At least if felt good."

"Elspeth." Rory grasped my wrist and tugged me towards him. "Don't ever say that. Power like ours isn't supposed to feel good. It's a blessing *and a curse*. Rely on it too much to fix things and you risk losing yourself to a darker calling." I blinked at him, my cheeks heating. "Do you understand?"

I nodded.

He turned and crossed the room. He picked up some pillows and tossed them into the centre of the space and gestured for me to sit.

I plonked my arse down and crossed my legs, feeling like a minnow in an ocean full of sharks.

Rory sat opposite and studied me for a long moment, making me squirm under his scrutiny. I trusted him, I liked him, I could talk to him, but in the end, he intimidated the crap out of me. I wanted to be good at this, but... *Elspeth, you haven't even tried yet.*

"You were bullied growing up?" he finally asked.

"I was small, unsure of myself, and shy," I told him. "That made me an easy target."

"So you made yourself invisible."

I nodded. "I could cope with that."

"It's clear that type of thinking followed you into

adulthood," Rory mused. "Now it's time to undo all of that. When you use your Colours, your intent has to be strong or your prisms won't hold."

"How do I do that?"

"By believing me when I say that you're special, Elspeth. You're kind, intelligent, and determined."

"How do you know that? You've only known me for a few days. I could be pretending."

"I can only tell you so much. You have to do the rest." He smiled and reached into his jacket pocket. "This is for you. You might not need it, but every Druid should have their own."

He handed me an ornate knife and I couldn't help but be confused. What was I supposed to do with this?

It was the size of a pen with a raw point of clear quartz set into one end and a small, razor-sharp, silver blade on the other. Delicate runes had been carved into the length, their meaning unknown.

"I saw others like this in the library," I told him. "What is it?"

"It's a nwyfre stele," he replied, pronouncing the unfamiliar word as noo-iv-ruh. "It's a tool used by young Druids to help seal their prisms. The crystal harnesses energy and the knife is for ritualistic bloodletting."

I made a face. "Ritualistic bloodletting?"

"It's not that dramatic," he said with a laugh. "Adolescent minds don't have the skill to reinforce the intent behind their Colours, so they use their blood to complete their prisms. You only need a drop."

"Thank you. I..." I turned the stele over in my hands and studied the shard of quartz. What would a drop of my blood do? I wasn't exactly a pure Druid.

Rory shifted before me. "What's wrong?"

"I..." I forced myself to look up at him. "What if my blood muddies things?"

"We won't know until we try. That's why we're training."

I didn't reply. Instead, I turned over the stele and ran my thumb over the runes. "What do they mean?"

"It's a prayer of sorts," he explained. "Before our people left the homeland, we had another language which is largely forgotten now, but we still use the runes."

"To anchor Colour in light switches and mysterious tattoos?"

"Yes." He poked the stele. "It means 'the blessing of earth, sea, and sky'. Thríbhís Mhór."

The time to try to access my Colour was fast approaching, but I still had a million questions. Maybe I was putting it off after my arm grew its own holographic crystals, but maybe preparedness was three quarters of the equation.

"What are the limits of a Druid's Colour? What can we do exactly?" I asked.

"Druids are linked to the fabric of nature, including the threads which create reality," Rory explained. "We can do just about anything with enough study and experience, but it always comes at a price," he tapped a finger on my temple, "mentally and physically."

"So I'm limited by my own strength?"

"Correct. There are ways to amplify Colour, like crystals, but there's always a limit. Strengthening the mind can also help, so does the simple passage of time."

I felt my brow furrow as I contemplated his answers. "Is it the same with the Chimera?"

"As far as we can tell, yes."

I guessed they weren't willing to divulge their weaknesses to the enemy, but if they were bound to the laws of nature, then it stood to reason they were limited in the same ways.

"And there are some Druids who can do different things like Jaimie?"

Rory nodded. "Those abilities are inherited through different family lines."

"Can you do anything special?"

"I'm a regular vanilla Druid."

He looked disappointed, but I still thought he was cool, so I told him.

"Let's try without the stele first," he said with a shake of his head. "As an adult, theoretically, you don't need it."

"Thank goodness. I wasn't looking forward to cutting myself." I loosened my shoulders. "So, what am I making?"

"Try something simple, like a flower. A lot of the ones you see in the Warren are made from prisms."

A flower? It seemed easy enough to imagine a daisy, but what about all the lines and angles I'd seen shimmering in Ignis' coat? I knew the cat was way more complicated—and light-years beyond my comprehension—but he was still made from the same basic Colour.

"How do I know what shape to make?" I asked, my brain almost exploding trying to figure it out. "Aren't prisms supposed to be complicated geometric patterns?"

"They are," Rory said, "but you don't need to worry about that. Your Colour understands your intent and forms around it. That's what creates the elaborate shapes. You don't need an equation or a ruler."

"You say it like it's simple and not totally weird." *Like I hadn't just found out magic existed a handful of days ago.*

"Because it is. It's who you are, Elspeth."

"Okay." I held out my hand, palm facing up. "So, do I just picture it in my mind and…make it grow?"

"See? You don't need a teacher."

I shook my head and pictured the first flower that came to mind—a daisy with a bright yellow centre and white petals. Simple, right?

I narrowed my eyes and instantly felt ridiculous.

"You're not trying to make your hand explode," Rory quipped. "Don't squint like that."

"*Shh,*" I hissed. "I'm concentrating."

A spark of warmth prickled in my palm, and to my surprise, a blue and purple drop sprung into life.

It gained form, shaping into lines and drew into a triangle, then sprouted another side to become three-dimensional.

"*I'm doing it,*" I said with an excited gasp.

"Concentrate," Rory coaxed. "Remember your intention and allow your Colour to form the prism."

Locking onto my mental image of the daisy, I willed the copy to grow in my hand. The triangle continued to grow, other lines and angles adding themselves to my first prism. Even curves and spirals sparked into existence, softening the hard corners.

My breath caught as blue and purple light began to solidify into a bright yellow centre with pure white petals. I was conjuring a flower from nothing. Scratch that…not nothing, from *Colour*.

"This is where it begins," Rory murmured. "Small steps this time."

I held my palm up to the light and tilted my head to the side, inspecting the forming daisy.

"I can't believe it…" Tears pricked in my eyes. "I did this. *Magic*."

"Without the stele, too…*and* it's pure Colour," Rory stated. "Nothing green about it."

"*Very funny*." I groaned as the flower sparked and began to dissolve, losing its shape as my concentration lapsed.

"And that's what happens when you don't finish a

prism," he added. "It crumbles and goes back to where it came from."

I watched in amazement as the Colour broke apart and faded into my skin like weightless glittering sand. *Cool.*

"I've been meaning to ask you something," Rory began, his expression taking the shine off my triumph.

"What?"

"You named your cat Ignis."

I curled my lip. "So?"

"Everything links back to your father's death. Is there a reason?"

"How should I know? The cat chose his name, I just gave him some suggestions." Awkward silence opened between us that I didn't like. "Yesterday you said people were talking about me. That there were rumours. What are they?"

"Elspeth, I don't think—"

"I know more than you think I do," I interrupted. "I'm a grown woman with little life experience, but I'm not blind. I can see the way people look at me. Vanora treats me like I'm a mutant, and I know it's not just because she's got some twisted genetic claim over you. Delilah said there are good Fae, but it doesn't seem to matter which one I am—I'm hated for being born anyway."

"It's not like that," he argued.

"It's *exactly* like that." I shook my head, my mood souring. "What are they saying?"

He sighed and lowered his gaze. "A woman who bridges the gap between Fae and Druid has the power to destroy both."

"I know all of that," I said with a scowl. "Painfully so."

"It's not just prejudice because of what the Chimera are doing to us, Elspeth. It was spoken in a prophecy."

I made a face. "So?"

"Prophecies might be nonsense in the human world, but they aren't in the Druid world. When a Druid has a vision, there is always truth in it."

"So I'm screwed in whatever I do? *Thanks for nothing*."

"Elspeth, prophecies aren't set in stone. What good would it be to see a possible future if it wasn't meant as a warning?"

If I knew anything about future visions from books and movies, is was that they were rarely that simple in the first place. At least they weren't one sentence of direct, legible English.

"But that's not all of it, am I right?" I asked, taking the chance he was holding something back.

From the look on his face, I'd hit the nail on the head.

"*Rory*."

His jaw tightened. "Born of ashes, dead in darkness, a soul who bridges the gap has the power to destroy Druid and Fae alike. When the black sun rises, death will choose the hand of fate."

"*That's nonsense,*" I hissed. "How do you know it's about me?"

"You bridge the gap between Druid and Fae. Your father died in a catastrophic fire which caused you to be born anew as a Druid…out of metaphoric ashes. Who else could it be about?"

"Dead in darkness?" I scoffed. "Black suns?" I didn't know what to believe.

"Don't let it get to you," Rory urged. "You have the power to be whoever you want to be. This is your chance to make your future the way you want it to be."

I sighed. "It's a beautiful notion, Rory, but this isn't high school. The stakes are higher than just getting good grades."

"Exactly. That's why you have to believe."

I can only tell you so much. You have to do the rest. But he could teach me how to fight. If he wanted me to believe, then I had to see for myself. I had to learn how to take my own life in my hands and keep my fate apart from those who'd use me to fulfil their crazy prophecy. If I was going to destroy anything, it would be of my own free will.

"You're right," I told him, closing my fist around my stele. "It is up to me, and as my *neach-gleidhidh*, I'm asking you to help me learn how to fight. I won't be a pawn in anyone's prophecy of destruction. My destiny is my own. No one else's."

He smirked and laughed. "You're still saying it wrong."

"Don't take my moment away from me," I retorted. "Will you help me or not?"

"I get to turn you into a badarse warrior woman?" He winked. "*Deal.*"

I closed my eyes, wondering yet again how I'd travelled so far from my barely passable life in Sydney to this. My once mediocre future seemed idyllic in comparison to what I now faced.

"This is only the beginning. It will only get tougher from here," Rory warned. "You'll hate me before long."

"I'd never hate you," I said, opening my eyes. "I'm bound to get angry and want to punch you in the face, but hate…? That's such a strong word." And I believed every word I said.

Rory studied me for a long moment, his lips quirking as he suppressed a smile. "Well, as long as we have our priorities straight." Then he leaned closer and murmured, "You know, my foot still hurts from the first time we met."

I laughed, remembering when I'd stomped on it outside of Greyfriars. "You deserved it."

"Ach, I need to work on introducing myself to people, especially in darkened graveyards."

"Cause that's not creepy at all."

"*My thoughts exactly.*"

"So, what *is* going on in the city?" I asked. "Has Owen come back yet? Has there been any trouble?"

"Ach, I wouldn't worry about it," Rory replied. "All that isn't important right now."

"I will worry about it," I snapped, my hackles rising unexpectedly. "All this trouble is because of me. If I'd known, maybe I could have avoided almost getting you killed. *Twice.*"

He snorted. "You didn't almost get me killed."

"That's not what I heard."

"*Ach, Vanora,*" he muttered.

I raised my eyebrows.

"Vanora has been watching the new Mrs. Campbell," he said. "And Jaimie's waiting for Owen's return…which is not in doubt. He'll be back and will waste no time looking for you."

"All the more reason to become a bad-arse warrior woman." I held up the nwyfre stele. "Where am I supposed to put this?"

"Ach, watch where you point that thing," Rory declared. "I've got a case you can put it in. Just don't poke anyone's eye out in the meantime."

13

Rory and I trained every day for the next week. He taught me what he knew about Colour and how to control it, and it wasn't long before I was making bouquets of flowers that held their shape—daisies, carnations, lilies, daffodils, roses, then onto miniature palm trees and spiky cacti.

For the first time in my life, I was good at something.

Rory also spent time showing me the basics of hand-to-hand combat, building my non-existent skill to something passable. I was tired and bruised, but I was showing the first signs of becoming stronger which only pushed me to want to do more.

I showed my face in the kitchen for breakfast and dinner, but even though I tried to smile and speak to the other Druids, no one met my gaze. Only Rory and Jaimie gave me the time of day, sitting with me to eat and walk through the Warren together.

Ignis joined us at mealtimes, eager to catch any random food scraps that fell onto the floor…or were snuck to him under the table. For a cat made up of prisms, he was rather fixated on food. He was the perfect pet in more ways than one—he didn't need to be fed or need a litter tray—but he had all the mannerisms of an arrogant feline. As we curled up together at night, I wondered who he'd been before his soul had shattered.

Things were going reasonably well until the day I woke up and my hair was completely green.

Rory definitely noticed, but he was gracious enough by now to know not to mention it—even when the mirrors in the training room reflected it back at me a thousand-fold.

"Illusions are more advanced but essential to our survival on the surface," Rory told me. "Technically, they're a type of portal—a bending of reality to render us invisible—but they also play on spiritual power."

"Spiritual power?" I asked. "What's that exactly?"

"It's the power of the mind. Spirit is linked to consciousness. Well, they're pretty much the same thing. We can wrap ourselves in a veil of reality, but it's only thin to avoid the Chimera from detecting us. To make it worthwhile and not break the moment someone looks in our direction, we need to trick the minds of those around us."

"We can do that? Alter people's perceptions?"

"Only a little." Rory shrugged. "Actually, it's a

genetic anomaly passed down to us from the first Spirit Walkers."

I thought about it for a long moment, twisting a lock of my green hair around my finger. The strands shone emerald, lime, pear, and olive.

"Maybe all Druids used to be Spirit Walkers," I mused. "A long time ago."

"Perhaps. No one really knows."

"You don't know your people's origins?"

"Do humans know how they evolved with one hundred percent certainty?" He smiled. "Some mysteries are too old to ever solve. Besides, it's *our* people, Elspeth."

I grimaced as we sat on the pillows. It was difficult enough trying to understand my new reality, let alone the origins of a supernatural race of people.

"So, what's it going to be today?" I asked, steering the subject back to my practical training. "Can I move on from plants yet?"

"I want you to try to make an illusion," Rory replied.

My eyebrows rose. "An illusion? Are you sure? I mean…it sounds complicated."

"It's not, really. It calls on the basic building blocks of a Druid's Colour. If you can master this, then you might be able to create a portal one day."

"Wait. I thought everyone could make portals?"

Rory shook his head. "Everyone has the power to, that's why we're so attractive to the Chimera, but not many have the skill required to open one."

"I feel like I've been tricked into thinking you're more awesome than you really are."

"*Harsh.*" He laughed, but then became uncharacteristically serious. "One day, I hope to master them."

I studied him for a moment, then asked, "So you can go to the Darklands?"

His gaze found mine, then he coughed, blinking away his expression. "Illusions," he stated. "Let's try together." He rose, gesturing to me. "Stand up and close your eyes."

I did as he said, allowing his expertise to guide me.

His hands found mine. "Now close out all outside sounds and focus on my voice." Our fingers entwined. "Find your Colours and bring them to the surface…*slowly*. Just a trickle."

I felt the now familiar warmth of my Druid abilities rise, the threads that formed the prisms I'd been diligently practicing shimmered and awaited my command.

"Good," Rory murmured. "Remember to focus on your intent. A faint curtain to separate you from the perception of those around you."

I let my intent entwine with my Colour and felt the air shift. Light played across the outside of my eyelids and I opened my eyes.

Rory was gone.

My expression faded into confusion as the training room faded and a thick fog twisted around my ankles. Whispers echoed from someplace far away, the words too faint and garbled to make any sense.

I felt myself slipping away and I began to panic. "Rory?"

Answering my call, he emerged from the mist and grabbed my hand, pulling me towards him.

"Don't worry," he said. "I've got you."

The training room came back into focus like he'd flicked a switch, and I stood there dazed.

"I wasn't supposed to do that, was I?" I managed to ask some time later.

He shook his head. "No, and if you'd gone any farther, I'm not sure I could have pulled you back."

I sucked in a shaky breath as my stomach gurgled. I felt like throwing up. "What did I do?"

Rory frowned, but didn't reply.

"That wasn't Colour, was it?" I whispered. "That was…Fae." A cold shiver prickled down my spine. "*Freak.*"

"Hey, you're not a freak. You're two for the price of one, okay?"

I snorted shook my head, my green hair fluttering. "Like a two-in-one shampoo and conditioner."

"She's making jokes," he said with a smile. "That's good."

Looking around the room, I wasn't sure what to do. When I'd stepped into the fog, it felt like I was out of control, like I'd set something into motion…

"C'mon," Rory said, placing his arm around my shoulders. "Let's go for a walk."

"I don't want to go out there." I sniffed and lowered my gaze. "I don't want them to see me rattled."

"I want to show you something," Rory said, pulling me against his side. "It's worth it, I promise."

I tucked my trembling hands into my sleeves and nodded. "If you say so, *neach-gleidhidh*."

"Well, colour me impressed. Your pronunciation is finally getting better!"

The library was empty when we walked in.

I gazed up at the amethyst dome, the sight of it taking my breath away just as it did the day I first met the Elders. Was it only a week ago? I felt like I'd gone through a metamorphosis that'd lasted years.

"These books hold the collective knowledge of the Druids," Rory said as we wandered past the shelves. "Well, the Druids who came through the Darklands. Knowledge is important to our people, so the first Druids wrote everything they remembered from the time before."

"The first Druids…like Delilah and Rowen?" I asked.

Rory nodded. "There are accounts of their journey through the Darklands and what they remember from their time on the other Earth. But there's more than that. There are books on botany, zoology, Colour, history, runes, languages… Also human books. There's a mean fiction section."

I laughed and ran my fingers over some of the spines. There had to be thousands of books here. How could so few Druids have written them? I supposed there was an eight-hundred-year window of productivity.

"You're welcome to read anything you like," Rory added. "Though it must be done within the library. The only books you can take out are the novels."

I walked the length of one shelf, reading the spines as I went. "Are there any on the Fae?"

"We didn't know of them until the Chimera showed up," he said with a frown. "So there isn't anything useful. The Fae were confined to Ireland until recently…as you know."

"Until the Witches opened the portals," I said so he knew I understood.

He walked around one of the display cases. "These are some of the things that were brought through the Darklands. Nwyfre steles, daggers, jewellery, crystals… All from the other Earth."

I joined him and studied them all, wondering if there was some kind of biohazard risk bringing things from another planet. Maybe it didn't matter considering they were the same place, just slightly different.

"Why are you showing me all of this?" I asked, looking up at him. "What does this have to do with what I did?"

"You're descended from a family with a rich heritage, Elspeth. All of this is a part of who you are. You are entitled to it, just as much as anyone else." He stepped closer. "I—" The library door opened with a loud creak, silencing him.

"There you two are," Jaimie declared, lumbering across the room. "When you weren't in the training room, I was worried you'd gone into the city."

"Ach, I know I like to bend the rules, but not that far," Rory complained. "What's the matter?"

"Nothing," Jaimie replied. "Delilah is looking for you." He turned to me and smiled. "And how are you getting along, eh? Graduated from flowers yet?"

"Well enough," I told him. "I'm starting on illusions."

He whistled and nudged Rory with his elbow. "Going hard, huh? Good for you."

"Tell Delilah I'll be along in a minute," Rory said, his brow creasing.

"Right." To me, he said, "Dinner?"

I grinned and nodded enthusiastically. "Same time, same place."

Jaimie waved a big hand at us and sauntered away. His easy-going nature was infectious and some of my anxiety began to ease. I wouldn't know what to do without those two Scottish rogues looking out for me.

My smile faded. *Dissolve.* That's what I'd do…like I'd almost done in the training room.

"Rory?" I asked, glancing at the library door. I

waited until Jaimie had closed it before I went on. "What did I do earlier?"

He bit his bottom lip. "You were… You were becoming *essence*."

I frowned, my brow furrowing so deep I felt a headache coming on.

"You were transcending to another reality," he added.

I stared at him, not quite grasping what he was saying. "I was Spirit Walking?"

"Yes and no…" He glanced around the library and pulled me into the alcove. "Elspeth, you were ascending."

"Ascending?"

"If I hadn't stopped you, you would have evolved." He grasped my shoulders. "Do you understand what I'm saying?"

I swallowed hard, my mind trying to grasp notions that were far beyond what I knew.

Ascension meant to rise beyond the physical. To have one's consciousness exist as pure energy. I got why he was so worried—if I broke free of my body, I might never come back to it.

I nodded, a knot of fear tangling in the pit of my stomach. I was concerned, too.

"I don't understand it," Rory murmured. "We have to be careful from now on, okay?"

"Okay," I managed to choke out.

"It'll be all right," he said, pulling me in for a hug. "I'll be there to help you."

I trembled in his grasp, my eyes wide and unseeing as I began to realise the depths of why the Druids and the Chimera were fighting over me.

It wasn't about being mixed blood. It was something more sinister.

Dead in darkness… *What was I becoming?*

Troubled by what I'd done, I skipped dinner and hid in my room.

I hadn't bothered to unpack my suitcase, but I sat before it and took everything out, folded it, and put it all back again. Zipping up my packing cubes, I revelled in the organised neatness—the only thing I seemed to have control over.

How tragic.

Holding out my palm, I studied the creases—the heart line, the life line, and the fate line were the only ones I knew. I was unlucky enough to not have a fate line. What that meant was a mystery.

A faint spark of Colour bloomed where the crease was meant to be, and I closed my fingers with a sigh.

Finally bored of my own downward spiral, I went to bed at a cringeworthy early time of eight-thirty.

I dozed at first, my mind swirling with a thousand images, then I fell into a deep slumber.

I stood in the close where I last saw Owen. I knew it was a dream, but something about it felt more real than a vision created by my subconscious.

Rain fell in light bursts, swirling then clearing as the wind buffeted across the rooftops four stories above. The stone underfoot was slick and tinted green where it met the houses. Delicate moss clung everywhere the dirt had gathered, even in tiny holes in the cobbles, giving away how damp Edinburgh was year-round.

Elspeth.

I turned at the ragged whisper, the sound of my name clawing painfully down my spine.

"Who's there?" I called, my dream voice echoing.

No one replied and I turned, crying out as I came face to face with Owen.

His face morphed between Fae and human as he sneered at me, his power palpable in the enclosed alley.

"They can't hide you forever," he sneered. "I'll come for you when the time is right and *nothing* will stop me." He held up a clawed hand and reached towards me.

I was frozen to the spot as the close shrank around us, pulling Owen closer.

Something wasn't right. I blinked, trying to force my feet to move, but they wouldn't budge. This didn't feel like a dream anymore. The rain was cool against my skin, the scent of damp stone filled my nose, and the power of the Chimera made me sick to my stomach.

It was real.

Run, Elspeth. Run.

Colour bloomed inside me and I turned with a cry. I sprinted up the close, leaping up the stairs, propelled by the power Rory had taught me how to harness. I careened out onto the Royal Mile with Owen's Dark presence on my heels and kept going.

The road was empty, the lack of human activity unsettling as I sprinted past St. Giles Cathedral.

"You can run, but I will catch you!" Owen shouted. "The Chimera will claim you, Elspeth. *It's in your blood.*"

A sharp pain scratched across my chest and I stumbled…

I woke with a start and found Ignis standing on top of me, his claws imbedded in my cleavage. Green eyes narrowed and he head-butted me with an enthusiastic meow.

Breathing heavily, I raised my hand and the crystal light began to glow softly, casting a faint, icy-blue hue over my room. I wrapped my arm around Ignis, glad he was there to wake me up.

"You knew," I whispered, leaning my cheek against his furry spine. "Owen was reaching out for me, wasn't he?"

His stripy tail flicked back and forth, his prisms sparkling.

"Rory was right," I murmured.

Every day I seemed to get closer to something, as if the day I almost killed Owen unlocked a terrible power inside me. Making prisms of plants was one thing, but ascending through the spirit world…? What did that even mean? The Chimera wanted to control me so badly that they just tried to reach me through the Druid's illusions.

What was it that Rory had told me in the library? Or, more importantly, what hadn't he said?

The more I thought about it, the more I realised he knew something. Why was he keeping it from me though? Had the Elders commanded him to stay silent?

"He knows something, Ignis," I said. "I think… I think he knows why my father left the Warren. I bet that's what he was going to tell me before Jaimie walked in."

The cat purred, blowing gusts of air out of his nose that made him sound like a snorting horse.

"Don't worry," I murmured, spearing my hand through his soft hair. "I'll get it out of him. I deserve to know the whole story. Especially now that they can reach my dreams." A curtain of green hair fell over my shoulder and covered Ignis like a mossy blanket. "It's my prophecy after all."

14

———

All I had were piles of questions with no answers…and so much green hair I didn't know what to do with it.

I looked at my reflection in the glossy walls of the Warren and sighed. *I guess you're a punk now, Elspeth. Maybe you should shave it into a mohawk.*

Walking into the main cavern, I looked up at *Salle*. The willow always looked like a painting to me, the rainbow of green, purple, and blue too magical to be real. Lately, my life had taken on the same sheen.

I spotted Ignis prowling along one of the branches, stalking a sparrow construct. He pounced, but the bird escaped his clutches with a swift flap of its wings. That was a metaphor if I ever saw one.

Sighing, I ventured to the kitchen.

I wanted to talk to Rory and warn him about Owen invading my dream, but as I scanned the tables, I realised he wasn't there. Jaimie wasn't either, but I knew he had other duties in the city. It must have been a late one if he was missing out on mealtime.

Gathering the last scraps of my withered courage, I crossed the room and picked up a tray from the mismatched pile at the end of the table. Still feeling guilty over my freeloading, I filled a bowl with a handful of muesli and stepped down the line.

"I see you've made yourself at home."

I bristled at the harsh tone in the unknown voice behind me and steeled myself.

"I'm speaking to you," the voice snapped.

The whole kitchen fell silent. I felt the pressure of the gaze of every Druid in the room piercing my back like hot pokers. Knowing I couldn't escape a confrontation, I turned.

It was Darby, the waifish woman with the pixie haircut I'd met the first day, and some other Druids I only knew from their passing glares. I'd given them less than appropriate nicknames because none of them were interested in introductions. They were butt face, arse crack, lemon sucker, and I thought I should stop there before I got bombed with one-star reviews…or accidentally revealed their new names to their faces.

"Can I help you?" I asked, forcing myself to speak.

"You stand there like you don't know what he did," she said, raking her gaze over me. "It's insulting."

"Who?"

"Your father."

I scowled. "What about him?"

"No one's told you?" She laughed and shook her head. "Typical. They'll do anything to protect the clueless half-blood over their own."

"What are you talking about?" I demanded. "If you've got something to say, *just say it.*"

"It's all his fault, Elspeth. The Chimera."

"You really hate me that much that you'll resort to lies?" I shook my head. "*Pathetic.* I never did anything to you or the Druids, Darby. I didn't ask for this." I fisted my hand into my hair and held it up. "*I don't want it.*"

"I'm not lying," she retorted. "Why would I need to when the truth is so much more powerful."

She stepped closer and glared. She was shorter than I was, but her presence was still intimidating. Darby was a Druid in full control of her Colour, and I felt it simmer along her skin as she faced-off with me.

"Your father meddled with things he was commanded to leave be," she said. "He fell in love with a Fae and created something that should never have been."

I swallowed hard. "But that would have been…"

"That's right," she declared with a sneer. "Before you were born."

In that moment, I felt incredibly stupid. I was twenty-five. My mother was a Fae. The Witches hadn't re-opened the portals until five years after I was born. The Fae who'd been trapped here were confined to Ireland and were nothing but withered husks without their power. My father must have opened portals to the Fae realm and… He…

"He brought the Chimera down on us," someone else said. "If it wasn't for him, they wouldn't be hunting us."

"And there wouldn't be children here without parents," Darby snarled.

"I— He'd never—" I didn't want to believe her. My father was kind, nurturing, and strong-hearted. He sacrificed his life to save people from environmental disasters. He fought bushfires. He…

"He betrayed all of us, Elspeth," Darby snapped. "Instead of facing trial and banishment, he stole you and ran like a *coward*."

"That's not true," I said, shaking my head. "He'd never—"

"Like he'd admit it," she spat. "He didn't even tell you the truth of what you are." Her gaze raked over me, her look of disgust made my skin crawl.

"You're lying."

"The longer you stay here, the more danger you put all of us in," Darby continued, ignoring my pitiful attempts at defending my father. "One misstep and you'll let the Chimera into the Warren and we're all dead or enslaved."

Anger welled in my heart, bringing a burst of unknown energy. *She is baiting me.*

"Evil is a choice and right now, you're pushing me

to make a really bad one,'" I snarled. "Is that what you want?"

She sniggered. "It wouldn't hurt to speed up the process of getting rid of you."

"I can't believe you."

"*Gordan Quarrie*. That wasn't his true name," she said like it meant something more than it was supposed to.

"True name?"

"Oh, hasn't Rory told you about that? Every Druid has a true name. Whoever knows it has power over your spirit. Only outside of the homeland, that is."

I didn't know if she was telling the truth or not, but I was going to buy into what she was trying to sell —which smelled like a whole lot of bull to me.

"Wouldn't it be useful if there was a ritual we could do to find out yours?"

I stared at her, flabbergasted. "How could you be so cruel?"

"It's nothing, really," Darby told me, "especially compared to the destruction you're destined to bring down on us."

I was numb.

She stepped closer, her cool gaze stabbing deep. "Be warned, Elspeth Quarrie. One misstep and you won't escape the consequences. *We will make you pay*."

My heart twisted as she walked past, knocking her shoulder against mine. I stumbled but was too shocked to say or do anything to retaliate.

Suddenly, I wasn't hungry anymore.

They didn't know me. I didn't want to be the centre of a prophecy of destruction. I didn't want to cause trouble or hurt anyone. Darby might be telling the truth about my father, but I didn't do those things. I wanted to help, but these people couldn't see past their prejudice. I got that they were angry, and they had every reason to be, but they should be blaming the Chimera—they were the ones hunting us.

Rage rose within me and I turned. Striding towards Darby as she walked away, I launched myself at her with a cry.

We fell to the floor and pummelled one another, my fists slamming into her face. She struck me, snarling with her own unbridled fury, but I was too enraged to stop.

Colour welled around us as the Druids gathered, watching in stunned silence.

"*Enough.*"

A shockwave vibrated through the kitchen, knocking everyone back a step. My fist halted mid-air as Darby's eyes widened.

Delilah loomed over us, her presence menacing to say the least. "Darby. Elspeth. *Stand.*"

We rose and at least I had the good grace to look embarrassed, Darby just jutted out her chin in defiance.

The Elder glared at Darby. "Report to Rowen."

She scowled. "But—"

"*Immediately.*"

The Druid hissed at me and wiped at her bloodied nose, then strode out of the kitchen.

"Elspeth," Delilah said, her expression unreadable.

I said nothing, waiting for the humiliation of her discipline to strike me down.

"Come with me."

Delilah's quarters were just as quirky as her fashion sense. It was also the last place I expected to find myself in the wake of my very first punch-up.

While I had a single bedroom, the Elder had a whole suite. The living room was adorned with art, shaggy rugs, a seventies-inspired beaded curtain, an enormous crystal geode in the corner, and a soft fabric couch with a multi-coloured, hand-crocheted, granny square blanket draped along the top.

While it was homely enough, I could still feel the hostile stares that had followed me out of the kitchen.

Closing the door behind her, she asked, "Is there an explanation for what happened in the kitchen?"

"I've been bullied my entire life," I told her. "It felt good to finally *fight back*."

"Brawling is not the way," Delilah stated. "There are times when raising arms is appropriate, but we never turn on our own."

"That's the thing though, isn't it? I'm not one of you. I'm not a Druid and I'm not Fae. I'm something in-between." I shook my head. "I'll forever be a symbol of what you lost. My father is dead and now I'm the only one left to blame."

Delilah said nothing, she simply waited for me to unload my anger on her.

"I thought Druids were supposed to be in tune with nature," I went on. "But all I see out there is a lot of poison."

"This world has changed us, Elspeth. I fear…" She looked at me, her expression troubled.

"You fear you were meant to die in the Darklands," I finished for her. "That this…*poison* is why you weren't worthy of returning home."

"We escaped, but perhaps we should have allowed the Old Ones to take us."

I didn't want to hear about her doubts. I wanted answers.

"Is it true?" I demanded. "Is my father to blame for the Chimera?"

Delilah frowned and gestured for me to sit. "Come," she said. "I will tell you the whole tale, but you must promise me something."

"I'm done making promises."

"Humour an old Druidess." She wiggled her fingers, her rings clacking together.

"Fine." Sighing, I sat beside her on the couch. "What is it?"

"You must promise me to remain calm."

"That's the worst thing to tell someone right before you drop a truth bomb on them."

Delilah smiled, her eyes crinkling around the outer edges. "Your fire reminds me of his," she said quietly. "He was passionate, too."

"I don't feel passionate," I muttered. "I've always been small…"

"Not anymore. You've awoken, Elspeth, and now your true self has come forth." She grimaced. "And all at once, it seems."

I'd been amongst the Druids for long enough to understand that there was a deeper meaning to what she'd just said. "Awoken?"

"Your father bound your abilities," she replied, "that much is clear. I do wonder if he included a little more into the ritual than he had intended, but perhaps he wanted it this way."

"I don't understand. He wanted me to be shy and awkward?"

"He *was* hiding you."

I groaned and pinched the bridge of my nose. *Dad…*

Delilah's Colours swirled. "Your father… Gordan. He was a gifted Druid. Perhaps one of the most powerful we've ever seen in this reality. His skill with portals was second to none." She smiled, though the edges were tinged with melancholy. "He was searching for the way to the Darklands, though he never found it."

"But he found a way to the Fae realm?" I asked.

She nodded. "How long he'd been travelling there, no one knew, but by the time we found out…it was too late." Her gaze turned towards the door as if she was looking into the past. "He returned one evening with a newborn baby in his arms. You were swaddled so tightly and sound asleep, content to be in his arms and nowhere else." I could have sworn a tear formed in her eye. "He came to me in secret and admitted the danger he'd awoken."

"The Chimera." *Oh, Dad…*

"What I'm about to tell you is what he told me that night." Delilah sighed. "He'd been visiting the Fae realm for months, studying their ways, learning about their people…and he met your mother. His folly was love, Elspeth. Nothing more, nothing less. A forbidden love between Druid and Fae. It's true they have their own factions and wars. Their own good and evil. Within their darker realms lie the Chimera. At their core, Chimera are power hungry fanatics and hunted them to the ends of their world for daring to challenge the fabric of nature."

I sucked in a shaky breath. "When they found out what he was—"

"They wanted his power above all else," she confirmed. "They took your mother and it was all he could do to spirit you away. He was pursued and followed into this reality…almost to our doorstep. The Chimera have hunted us ever since."

"And the Witches made it easier for them."

"Yes, though I believe they don't know about us, let alone our plight."

"So, did the Chimera came after my parents

because of the prophecy?" I asked. "It wasn't only the Druids who foretold this, was it?"

"Yes, Gordan believed so. We both knew what a child of both worlds might be capable of one day, but there was no way to be sure. You were barely three days old. Neither of us could abandon you, especially not your father. Together, we decided to bind your abilities, allow you to be raised as a human child away from all of this. Prophecy is a fickle art…as is the meaning of the words spoken."

"Of course, it is." I shook my head, still bewildered by the notion that people went to war over so-called prophecies. "Did Dad tell you who my mother was?"

Delilah shook her head. "He felt it better to keep her identity a secret. The less people who knew the truth, the safer she would be…if she was still alive."

I sank back into the soft pillows on the couch, trying to let everything sink in. Darby was right, but there was more to it than a simple betrayal. It was like people always said—there were two sides to every story. I wondered what my mother's side was, but all I had were the secondhand scraps Dad had told Delilah right before he disappeared with me.

"You let him go, didn't you?" I murmured. "You helped him escape justice so he could hide me from the Chimera."

Delilah dabbed at her eyes with the sleeve of her flowing shirt. She didn't say it, but I took it as a confession.

"Who was he to you?"

"Gordan was my son," she replied. "And you are Elspeth Odhweine, my granddaughter, named for my mother, Elspeth...Spirit Walker."

Spirit Walker. The puzzle pieces began to click into place, though many were still missing. What I'd done yesterday with Rory might not be as Fae as I'd first believed.

"Why didn't you tell me?" I whispered.

"We were uncertain of your reaction. Your Fae heritage is a mystery to us, Elspeth, and coupled with Gordan's binding, we just couldn't take the risk. If you'd lost control, there was a chance the expulsion of power could have killed you and drawn the entire Warren into death itself." She smiled and placed a reassuring hand on mine. "Believe me when I say, this was not the way I wanted you to find out."

I knew she was telling me the truth. I didn't want it to be this terrible, but it was what it was. The Chimera hunted the Druids because Dad tried to find a way to get his people home but fell in love with a Fae along the way.

Through no one's fault, I was a symbol of the calamity that'd followed. The prophecy was just the gleaming cherry on top—and a target to lay blame upon. It was a wonder Delilah had held her role as Elder to be honest, but I doubted the others knew that she'd helped us escape. I decided it was best to keep that revelation to myself.

What did I do now? Continue to train? Ask to

have my powers bound? Disappear so the Druids and the Chimera could never find me? Was I meant to choose a side and wait for the black sun to rise?

"*I have the power to help,*" I murmured, remembering Dad's words. "*And when the Earth and her creatures cry out in pain, we should answer with our whole hearts.*"

"That sounds familiar," Delilah murmured.

"It was one of the last things Dad told me before he died." I worried the hem of my jumper. "He was leaving to go fight the bushfires west of Sydney and I wanted him to say home. He embraced me and said those words. He had the power to save lives and he went…but the Chimera finally caught up with us."

Delilah drew me close, winding her arm around my waist. "He loved you, Elspeth. He gave up everything to keep you safe."

But at what cost?

"You have his eyes, you know," she added. "Gordan always took after his father, but I suspect you take after your mother."

"I always wondered," I murmured. "What happened to your husband? My grandfather?"

"Lost to the Darklands."

"Oh…" My cheeks flushed. "I'm sorry."

"Don't worry," she told me. "It was a long time ago."

We sat together for a moment, both of us a little overwhelmed.

"What do I do now?" I asked. "I'm not exactly flavour of the month around here."

"The Druids have fear in their hearts," Delilah replied. "They will not be easily won, but we have a chance to set things right…if that's the course your heart wants to take you."

"We?"

"You, myself, and Raurich."

I cringed. "Rory knows?"

"He is your *neach-gleidhidh*. Of course, he knows." Now I knew what he was about to spill in the library yesterday.

"Does he know you're my grandmother?"

She smiled and smoothed my emerald hair behind my ear. "He does."

I sighed as an unfamiliar feeling of knowing settled over me. I should be angry, but I was calm instead, the earlier anger I'd felt towards Darby was a distant memory—though she was unlikely to forget any time soon.

"Will you help with my training?" I asked.

"It's best I keep my distance," she told me. "Let Raurich guide you, Elspeth. He is wiser than he realises, and I doubt you two met by accident."

I thought so, too. Speaking of Rory…

"The Chimera tried to reach me in my dreams last night," I said, remembering what I was so eager to talk to him about this morning. Dream invasions seemed to pale in comparison to what I'd just been told. "At least, I think they did. It felt so real…"

Delilah looked troubled. "Perhaps it's possible. There is so much we don't know about their power. Your Fae blood may give you some ability to connect."

That didn't sound good, but at least I was aware of it.

"Ignis woke me," I added. "It was as if he sensed them and pulled me out before it could go too far."

"My goodness." She chuckled and shook her head. "That cat has a knowing I've never sensed in a construct before. His soul must have led a special life before it found itself within my grasp."

"He certainly is a strange cat."

We sat in silence for a moment, both of us exhausted in our own way.

"I think we've had enough revelations for one day and you've missed a crucial morning of training," she told me. "It's time for you to return to your duties."

I rose with a nod, my heart lighter but no less troubled. I'd learned a great deal today, but the finer details of my birth had been lost along with my father. Perhaps my mother might still be alive, but there was zero chance of finding her.

Delilah coughed, drawing my gaze.

"Unfortunately, as Elder, I cannot let you go unpunished for your display in the kitchen," she stated. "I will leave the details to your *neach-gleidhidh*. No doubt he will be looking for you in order to do so."

I groaned and averted my gaze as my cheeks

heated. No doubt Rory would think of something mortifying.

"Elspeth?"

I managed to return my gaze to Delilah's.

"Keep your mind sharp, granddaughter," she murmured. "They will try again."

15

———

"I leave you alone for five minutes and you go and get yourself into a fight."

I looked up at Rory and scowled. *Salle* towered above us, its branches fluttering in the non-existent wind.

"The whole Warren is talking about it," he added, sitting beside me on the snarled tree root. He laid his coat across his lap and I wondered where he'd been.

"I feel like a fool," I muttered. "All this time I've been trying to understand this place, I've been clueless about the real reason people hate me… I know the truth now, but it cost me everything."

"I wouldn't go that far," Rory told me. "People make mistakes."

"I should have been told straight up."

"There was a good reason we didn't."

"I didn't explode, Rory. I'm a grown woman. I only explode into crystals when my life is threatened."

"Not exactly, huh?" He tilted his head to the side. "It was a different kind of explosion."

I glared at him, then swatted his hand away when he went to touch my face.

"You've got a black eye, you know."

I straightened up with a gasp. "*Have not.*"

"Have too. Makes you look tough."

I prodded at the skin around my eye. "I don't feel tough."

"You gave Darby a matching shiner and almost broke her nose."

"*God,*" I groaned, burying my face in my hands.

"Don't worry, she's been healed. I can help you with that eyeball situation if you want." He knocked his shoulder against mine. "You don't have to walk around looking like a pirate."

"You can do that?" I asked, my voice muffled by my palms.

"Aye."

I sighed, wondering if it would count for anything with the Druids if I refused and made my eye heal the old-fashioned way.

"Leave it," I said, letting my hands fall away. "Darby may have deserved a punch in the face for what she said to me, but I shouldn't have hit her like that."

"I was hoping you'd say that."

"Why?"

"With us Druids it's about the journey and the lesson attached to it, not the prize at the end."

"Well that's anti-climactic."

He smiled and looked up at *Salle*. "It's what makes us wise."

I followed his gaze, watching the prisms shimmer around the weeping branches. It was strange how it was becoming more and more familiar as the days wore on—like a magical tree was an every day occurrence. Did that mean I was finally accepting who I was?

"Rory?"

"Ach, here comes another barrage of questions," he said with a chuckle.

"Delilah said I was an *Odhweine* and that my great grandmother was a Spirit Walker. Is that true?"

"Of course, it's true," he huffed. "What you did yesterday was exactly that…" he trailed off, and Rory never trailed off.

"But?"

"But it doesn't change what you were becoming," he murmured, glancing at some Druids who were gathered on the other side of *Salle*.

That didn't sound good. I picked at my fingernails, scraping gunk from underneath them—a nervous habit.

"You and Delilah were alone for a long time." He looked at me like he was expecting me to tell him my assessment of her story.

"It's a lot," I told him. "My mother might still be alive, but I doubt it. The Chimera likely murdered her decades ago. If anyone could tell me what I'm becoming, it'd be her." I sighed. "Dad never talked about her. *Ever.* I always assumed she died and it was too painful for him to speak about. I resented it, but I also respected his loss. I never knew her, so I had a detachment to it, I guess."

"She might still be alive," he said.

"In another world where the door is guarded by the Irish Witches. Dad was the only one who knew the way."

"A technicality." He looked me over. "You're going to need a coat," he said out of nowhere.

"A coat? Where are we going?"

He wouldn't say as we went back to my room. I snatched up my leather jacket and tartan scarf, my curiosity spiking. We couldn't be going outside—the Elders had forbidden it.

Rory led me thorough the Warren, past familiar rooms and angry faces, before ushering me into a new section of the tunnel. There weren't any people here, and the doors that were open revealed boxes and crates stacked behind them. I wondered if this was supposed to be the Druid's version of storage lockers.

Finally, he swept his hand over a rune carved into the wall and a portal flared to life. He didn't hesitate to walk through it, so I followed him without question.

On the other side, I found myself standing in another kind of stone room. The turquoise and obsidian walls of the Warren were gone, and in their place were large grey blocks.

"This used to be part of the Old Town," Rory

told me. "A forgotten stairway leading into old tunnels leading towards Castle Hill. The rock was too difficult to dig far, so it was abandoned pretty quickly. It was intended to be a secret escape route from the castle in the Middle Ages, but when it was rediscovered it ended up becoming storage for body snatchers."

"Body snatchers?"

"Edinburgh was well known for its College of Surgeons and selling cadavers in backdoor deals was big business. A little stone room is a great place to hide stolen bodies waiting to be transported. It's like a miniature refrigerator."

I shivered. "Stolen bodies?"

"Oh, aye. People used to stake out cemeteries for funerals so they could dig up fresh bodies. It even escalated to the point where people were being murdered." He wiggled his eyebrows up and down. "The price of medical advancement, huh?"

He turned and pushed open an old wooden door. "We've hidden it with illusions, so it's a little piece of forgotten history. Edinburgh is full of it though, so the historians won't miss this little old-timey meat locker."

My stomach rolled and I let out a *humph* of disgust.

"This is our way to the surface," Rory said.

I peered through the door and glowered at the spiral staircase beyond. It was narrow—only wide enough for one person to squeeze inside—and rose steeply upwards. The three steps I could see were stone and the centres were so worn, they were shiny and dipped in the middles. An old rope was woven into iron loops and disappeared up into the gloom.

"It's eighty-nine steps to the surface," Rory said. "Think you can make it?"

"We're going into the city? Are you sure that's a good idea?"

"Are you questioning your *neach-gleidhidh*?" he asked with a wicked glint in his eye.

Somehow I knew this trip wasn't sanctioned, especially after that stunt I'd pulled, but Rory was right. He was my *neach-gleidhidh* and I wouldn't be the only one getting into trouble if we were caught. By now, I was well aware that Rory loved to break the rules.

"All right," I said. "Lead the way."

I climbed the stairs behind him, the enclosed space and the upward spiral making me dizzy. By the time we reached the top, I regretted letting him take me out the back way.

Rory opened a trapdoor and cold air blasted into the confined space. Once he was out, he held out his hand to help me up the last few steps into another confined space above.

As I caught my breath, I looked around and was stunned to realise we stood behind a mausoleum like the ones I'd seen on my fateful trip to Greyfriars. In fact, I was pretty sure that's where we were.

The sky was almost fully dark, which meant it was late afternoon in the Scottish winter.

"So, this is why you and Jaimie were here the

night I was attacked," I murmured. "You were simply passing through."

"The Thursday before last," Rory stated, counting the days on his fingers. "Fourteen days."

I turned and stared at him. "Is that all?"

He winked. "Time feels all messed up when you're living in a magical crystal cave."

I breathed deeply, equal parts thrilled and terrified to be outside again. This was where I first encountered the Chimera, after all.

"Why are we here?" I glanced at Rory. "Isn't this reckless? What if the Chimera are watching the kirkyard?"

"Someone I know is going to hide us behind one hell of an illusion." He looked at me pointedly.

"You want me to try another illusion out here?" I cried. "Weren't you there the last time?"

"You know how to do it, Elspeth," he told me. "Just don't be so heavy-handed, okay?"

Heavy-handed? Wasn't that what he was doing right now? I muttered under my breath and rolled my shoulders back and stretched my neck. *I thought I was being careful.*

"Fine," I said. "Just be on standby, okay?"

I closed my eyes and let my Colours rise. First a drop, then another until I had a small strand ready to weave. Then I allowed my intent to entwine with the little thread and cast the illusion out.

I felt the air shift and Rory slapped me on the shoulder.

"See?" he declared. "I knew you could do it with a little incentive snapping at your heels."

"Did I do it?"

"Aye. Perfectly."

I grinned, my heart feeling happier than it had in a long time. "You knew, didn't you?"

"That your abilities would thrive with a little added danger?" he asked. "Of course. I'm smart like that." He tapped his temple as if to seal the deal. "Now, I want you to maintain the illusion. This time, you'll get to see Greyfriars without the threat of multiple abductions."

I groaned, "*Rory*."

"Too soon?"

"No," I murmured, "just long enough."

"I must say, you're taking to your Colours like a duck to water," he told me as we emerged from behind the mausoleum and into a row of gravesites. "Your father was gifted, too. Or so I hear."

My excitement faded and I traced my fingertips over a name carved into the stone beside me. Above, a sculpture of a weeping angel looked down on us, her wings drooping low.

"We told each other everything," I murmured, looking up at the statue. "How didn't I know he was keeping such a huge part of himself hidden?"

"He was trying to protect you," Rory replied, "that much is clear. And I don't think it was just to keep you from falling into the hands of the Chimera."

I looked at him. "The Elders?"

"The other factions of Fae, perhaps," he replied.

He was still fiercely loyal to the Elders, and I couldn't blame him. They were his people. But were they mine? Delilah was my grandmother, but Rory, Jaimie, and Ignis had become my people. It wasn't because they were Druids or blood relations, it was because they had good hearts.

"How old are you?" I asked.

"Of all the things you could have asked me, that's what you want to know?"

"Humour me."

"Twenty-nine human years, though in Druid years, I'm like a toddler."

"So, the opposite of dog years."

"*Ouch.*" He clutched his chest, acting as if I'd struck him in the heart. "You're a right comedian."

I laughed and looked across the kirkyard.

"I can guess your age. Twenty-five."

"That's cheating," I complained.

"Can't help common knowledge."

An awkward silence fell between us—though I knew it was all on me—and I began to wander down the path, studying the gravesites and mausoleums. I hadn't had the chance to see much the first time and while Rory was with me, it seemed safe enough to linger.

I thought about the things Delilah had revealed. How my dad found the Fae realm. I wondered what it was like there and how he'd met my mother. What was she like? Did I look like her? Maybe she had the same brilliant green hair I did.

Suddenly, I found my thoughts drifting to Rory.

"Where are your parents?" I asked. "You don't talk about them."

"They died when I was a bairn."

"Oh…" I stopped and he stood beside me, his hands buried deep into the pockets of his coat. "I'm sorry, I didn't know…"

"Seems we have more in common than you first realised."

"Why didn't you mention it? I've been going on and on about my dad like an insensitive jerk."

"That's okay. It's still fresh for you. Besides, I don't like to talk about myself much," he admitted. "Though I like talking to you. Strange, isn't it?"

"It is," I agreed. "I feel the same way."

I read the inscription on the nearest headstone to keep my mind from clouding over with regrets and apologies. I doubted Rory would want them. *Sacred to the Memory of Thomas Riddell Esq. of Befsborough, in the County of Berwick, who died in Edinburgh on the 24.th Novm. 1806, aged 72 years.*

"It was the Chimera," he said after a moment. "It was when they first came to Edinburgh. I was three at the time."

I froze, even though I suspected that was going to be his answer. He had every reason to hate me as much as the other Druids, perhaps more, but here he was…the only person I could trust.

"I'm sorry," I murmured. "I—"

"It's no one's fault but the Chimera's," he interrupted, his tone kind. "You didn't strike them down."

"I get that, but people need someone to blame. My father brought them here because he was trying to save me. That's plenty of reason without all the other stuff. Why would you help me? It can't be because I'm also a Druid."

"When I said that to you, I meant it," Rory told me. "And I still mean it."

"The Elders want to use me as a weapon against the Chimera," I stated. "They want to take control of the prophecy before anyone else can."

"I know what you're trying to insinuate, Elspeth," Rory said, "and I deny it. We all want what's best for our people, but I also want what's best for you."

"And what's best for me?" I whispered.

He didn't reply straight away. We stood in the middle of Greyfriars for what felt like an age, the wind stirring my hair and chilling my bare fingers. The sound of Edinburgh traffic was a dull hum in the background and the lights of Castle Hill shone orange and white through the haze of a descending frost.

Finally, he gave me an answer.

"Choice," he said. "Everyone deserves a choice, especially you."

I lowered my gaze, embarrassment flooding my cheeks.

"Are…are we okay?" I managed to stutter.

"We're good, Elspeth. Nothing has changed between us."

I sighed in relief. "Good, you're the only person I trust around here. If I lost you…"

Something unknown flashed across his features, but it was so fleeting I wondered if it was just my insecurities manifesting.

"Don't fash, lass," he said, his accent thickening. "You don't have to worry, but there is one thing I have to do that you're not going to like."

I winced. "Dare I ask?"

"We have to settle the matter of your punishment."

"Damn, I hoped you'd forgotten about that."

"Not a chance, lass. Not. A. Chance."

16

The kitchen was more modern than I expected.

The cook stood before me, assessing me with a cool gaze. He looked middle-aged with his greying hair and lined face, but time was deceptive when it came to Druids. He could be over a hundred for all I knew.

"I'm Arnold Elinian," he told me, crossing his muscled arms over his chest.

"Elinian?"

He snorted with annoyance. "Elder Shor is my cousin."

I didn't think it was in my best interest to answer, so I waited.

"It's not my choice to have you here, but Rory insisted. You disturbed the peace of my kitchen and now you must restore it." He jabbed a finger at the sink, which was piled with dishes, trays, and various pots and pans.

My eyebrows rose and I asked, "By washing the dishes?"

"*And* the ovens." He kicked the toe of his boot against the door. "Don't forget the grease traps."

Druids struck me as the vegan type, so why they even had a grease trap was beyond me. I hadn't seen a scrap of meat since I'd been down here.

"Plant-based oil," the cook said, reading my expression. "Hot chips are a universal delicacy."

I looked at the oven as if it'd jump up and bite me. "Isn't there a prism for this?"

Arnold gave me an offended look and shook his head. "Colour isn't intended for household chores, *girl.*" He turned and picked up an apron from the table and threw it at me. "The sooner you begin, the sooner you leave."

I caught the apron against my chest and nodded. Sounded good to me, but I knew he didn't intend for it to sound like an incentive. He wanted me to leave because I was nothing but trouble.

The cook sighed at my stationary form and clicked his fingers. "Snap to it, girl. Lunch is less than four hours away and we need those trays."

Well, no time like the present. I picked up a bottle of dishwashing liquid and squirted it into the sink. Yellow soap pooled in the bottom and the lemony scent filled my nostrils. At least it was going to smell nice…until I reached the grease trap.

I was about to turn on the tap when a boom echoed from above, making the entire kitchen shudder. Pots and pans clattered as they swayed, and the cook set down the knife he was holding. The other Druids stopped what they were doing and looked at the ceiling as another boom shook the Warren.

"What was that?" I looked up, a growing feeling of dread blossoming in my stomach.

"Chimera!" someone called out from the hallway. "The Chimera are trying to break the portals!"

The dishwashing liquid bottle slipped from my fingers and fell into the sink. "The Chimera? Here?"

Arnold glared at me and opened his mouth to reply, but a commotion made him fall silent.

"*There she is! Take her!*"

I turned just as Vanora grabbed my arm.

"What are you doing?" I demanded. "What's going on."

"You friends are here," she snarled, "*Fae.*"

"But—" The words died in my throat when she slapped me, her palm cracking against my cheek.

"*Dùin do ghob*," she hissed. "You're going to face the consequences, Elspeth Quarrie."

I was dragged from the kitchen, Vanora's grasp biting into my arm. Druids stepped back as we passed, none of them speaking up for me. They began to follow, their hatred growing with every step.

"Vanora, stop," I cried. "What's going on?"

"*I said shut up,*" she hissed as we emerged into the main cavern. "The Chimera are at our door, just as you planned, *Fae.*"

The Druids gathered around *Salle*, shouting angrily as Vanora dragged me across the cavern.

"You've got this all wrong," I pleaded. "I didn't bring anyone here. I wouldn't—"

"Shut up, *bò bhrònach*," she hissed. "You have no voice here."

She shoved me away and I stumbled, falling against the willow.

Prisms ignited, wrapping around my wrists and twisting around my legs and middle. I cried out as I was forced against *Salle*, my back scratching painfully against the trunk. My arms were wrenched out to my sides and my feet were bound together by biting threads of Colour.

When I raised my head, I withered underneath the hateful glares of dozens of Druids.

Darby stood before me, her malice adding to my rising fear. "The Warren has been our sanctuary for eight hundred and fifty years, and she's been here barely a month and we face losing it to the Chimera! We should have never taken her in!"

Calls of agreement added to the crackling energy holding me in place, and I felt the searing burn of Colour dig into my flesh.

It wasn't supposed to be like this. Colour wasn't meant to harm… I struggled to hold onto my tears and squash down my panic.

"Gordan should have never gone through those portals!" Darby screamed. "He brought this calamity down on us by bringing *her* into this world!" She whirled, the back of her hand striking me across the face.

My head snapped to the side and for a moment, I felt nothing. Then all at once, stars bloomed in my vision and pain ripped through my cheek. Warmth trickled down my skin and I knew I was bleeding.

I am on trial…one I could never hope to win. Just like a witch in the Dark Ages, if I drowned, I was innocent and if I revealed my power, I'd be burned alive. Either way, I was doomed.

Was this what it had come to? Violence? Druids were meant to nurture. They were meant to be wise… But I knew I was right when I told Delilah that a poison had taken root in their hearts. The Darklands had been denied and this was the cost.

Colour rose within me, but it wasn't the only power that simmered underneath the surface. The threads I'd used to weave all those flowers were waiting for me to call, but so was the unstable force that had almost taken away my essence.

This was lightyears beyond the bullying I'd endured in high school. I wanted nothing more than to unleash my wrath upon the Druids, but I would do nothing. Violence was not the way.

Taking a deep breath, I returned my gaze to the Druids. If I fought back, I would give them exactly what they wanted—a reason to feed me to the wolves.

"What a pathetic creature," Vanora said, her lip curling into a sneer.

"She can't even speak up." Darby sniggered. "She knows she's guilty."

"She can't even protect herself. She has to rely on us to do it for her."

"No more," Darby added, raising her hand. Colour bloomed in her palm and I steeled myself.

"*Enough!*"

The sound of Rory's enraged voice echoed through the cavern, causing the Druids to fall silent. Vanora turned, her dark hair flying around in a whirlwind of anger. Darby glared at me and followed suit, standing before me.

Rory strode up the path, his expression wild, his body crackling with electrified Colour. His gaze fell on me and he didn't bother to conceal his shock. It must be bad, but I didn't feel anything.

"What is wrong with you?" he demanded. "This is not who we are!"

"The Chimera are at our door, Rory," Vanora replied, holding her head high. "She brought them upon us, and you stand there, *protecting her?*"

"Elspeth did nothing to warrant this kind of barbaric treatment," he cried. "We're not monsters, Vanora. *We're not the Chimera.*"

"It's about time we stepped out of our hole and took the fight to them," Darby said. "The old ways aren't working. We aren't a peaceful people anymore. We cannot allow her to complete the prophecy."

"By whatever means necessary." Vanora took a

step towards Rory. "You know I'm speaking the truth."

I breathed deeply as his gaze flickered to mine. The prisms hissed as I moved, burning into my wrists.

"Maybe the Old Ones were right to have the Darklands claim us," Rory snarled. "We don't deserve the homeland…not if this is how we treat our own."

"That's the thing," Vanora said, "she's *not one of us*."

"She's Fae," Darby declared. "And her blood will win out." She pointed to the ceiling. "*It's already happening*."

"She's also a Druid," he cried. "She's one of us whether you like it or not."

"She can never be one of us," Vanora snarled. "Not while she carries the blood of a Fae."

"You do realise if she's turned away, the Chimera will take her powers and use them against us. They will be able to open our portals, ravage the Warren, and then they will turn on the human world. You'll be sending her to her death and condemning us to ours."

Darby wrenched her knife from the scabbard tied to her waist, the blade ringing out as it slid against the leather. "Then we end it here for the greater good. *The black sun will never rise*."

My gaze lingered on the knife, my heart twisting in fear.

"*Don't*," Rory warned.

Darby spun and stabbed the blade towards my chest. In that moment, I thought my life was supposed to flash before my eyes, but all I saw was the Druid's hate as she bore down on me.

I didn't see my dad or catch a glimpse of the house I left back in Australia. I didn't see the happy moments I'd shared with Dad as a child, or the relief I felt every time he came home from fighting a bushfire. All I saw was the tip of Darby''s knife as it plunged towards my chest.

Colour exploded around me and Darby was thrown backwards, the knife clattering to the stone floor of the cavern.

I gasped, but the pain I'd been expecting never came.

Footsteps rang out as a blurred figure approached and the prisms holding me dissolved. I fell to the floor with an unbidden cry of pain, my wrists burning as I caught myself. My hair slipped forwards, covering my face from the gathered crowd.

"*This is not the way of the Druids*," Delilah boomed, the anger in her voice shaking the cavern. A few leaves fluttered in the air, the vibrations of her wrath dislodging them form *Salle's* branches and they stetted around me.

"*We do not harm our own*," she went on, leaving me silently weeping on the ground. "*And we do not act without the blessing of the Elders*."

Delilah must have made a gesture because Rory was beside me in an instant. His hand grasped my shoulders, but I wrenched myself away with a violent jerk. The sudden movement made fire erupt through my body, the burns from the prism making themselves known.

"The enemy is outside our sanctuary, but they cannot enter," Delilah continued. "While you bicker amongst yourselves and lay blame on a girl who came to us for help, the Chimera inch closer. Save your Colour for *them, for they are finally at our door.*" The silence was so thick, it weighed on my shoulders. "Druids, prepare for battle."

Commotion erupted in the cavern, spreading through the Warren. Druids began to move, leaving *Salle* at the Elder's behest. If anything, they were loyal…to a fault.

"*Elspeth,*" Rory murmured.

"Get off me," I snapped, pushing to my feet.

Ignoring the pain and the lingering stares of the Druids, I fled the cavern, not daring to look back.

No one stopped me. Delilah had spoken and there were more important things to do right now than to strike me down where I stood.

I shoved open the door to my room and slammed it closed behind me. I paced, my body throbbing as I pushed up my sleeves. My hands shook violently as I saw the burns had dug into my flesh like red angry slashes. It looked as if… It… At least they weren't bleeding.

They hated me. They wanted to kill me. Why? What did I do?

Nothing. I did nothing. My only crime was existing.

I cried out and grabbed my stele off the dresser

and threw it at the wall, the force of my rage pushing Colour with it. It rang out as it imbedded into the stone and I grasped my throbbing side.

The Chimera were here because of me. I might not have led them here, but it was me they wanted. If I wasn't here, then they'd follow me and leave the Druids alone. Rory and Jaimie… They would be safe, and the others could continue their hateful lives in peace.

Suddenly, I remembered the dream I had the first night I arrived in Edinburgh. *What are you doing here? Get out! Run before it's too late!*

"*Dad*," I whispered. I was a Spirit Walker; Delilah had said it herself. Dad *had* been trying to warn me.

I continued to pace, my rage building. I was powerless. I had nothing to offer. I didn't know who I was or what I was capable of. I was useless.

I lashed out, my fist flying towards the closet door, but instead of my knuckles colliding with hard wood, my outstretched arm blurred, passing through layers of reality and becoming transcendent…and passed straight through the solid door.

I pulled back, holding my hand against my chest, the anger shocked completely out of me.

Was it my Fae power? *It had to be.* I wasn't ascending, I was… I didn't know the name for it, not yet, but I understood now.

It was how I was going to escape.

I grabbed my jacket and scarf, snatching my little coin purse and passport out of my bag. Shoving them into the inside pockets of my coat, I threw it on and knotted the scarf around my neck. Doubling back, I found my fingerless gloves and beanie. At least I had the good sense to remember it was winter outside.

I had to leave while I still had the chance. The Warren was in an uproar, so if I was quick—

A loud meow echoed through my room as Ignis appeared out of thin air and began to move in figure eights through my legs.

"No, Ignis," I murmured, wiping at my tears, "you have to stay here. I can't protect you out there, okay? Stay with Rory. He'll keep you safe."

The cat yowled in protest, tapping his paw on my leg.

"It's me they want," I murmured, kneeling and scratching behind his ears. "Once they realise the Druids cast me out, they'll leave them alone. The Chimera will follow me to the ends of the Earth to possess my power. They won't come back here."

Ignis head-butted my hand, purring loudly. He was a special cat and his human soul was a rare and precious thing if he cared about a broken outcast like me. Delilah was right about that at least.

"Don't worry, I won't let them catch me. Rory taught me well."

With that, I rose and took a deep breath. *I hope this works.* Getting stuck inside a block of volcanic rock would suck.

Calling on my power, I phased through the wall… and into the city above.

17

Hurrying down the narrow close, I pulled my beanie down over my green hair and huddled into my jacket.

When I'd phased through the wall, my clothes and everything in my pockets had come with me—a handy side effect. I'd also landed in the courtyard of Edinburgh Castle, giving me another clue as to the range of my unknown abilities. I hadn't simply walked through a wall and emerged on the other side.

Maybe I teleported. Folding reality like the Druids did with their portals and dematerialising to another location with my Fae magic. Seemed logical, or as logical as things got in a world full of witches, fairies, and shapeshifters.

What *was* the term for Druids? Mage? It didn't seem to matter anymore.

Luckily, no one seemed to notice a green-haired woman appear out of nowhere. The horde of tourists taking selfies with the castle behind them were too busy trying to get their pout and the castle in the same shot. Still, I managed to cast an illusion around myself, just like Rory taught me.

I hastened down the stairs, emerging from the close and finding myself on the southern side of Castle Hill. I hadn't sensed anyone following so far, but I wasn't an expert.

Turning onto Grassmarket—it wasn't called a street or a terrace or a road, just Grassmarket—I found myself amongst a swathe of tightly packed market stalls. Some were selling arts and crafts, others wine and spirits. Local farmers were hawking organically grown produce, a man was selling pastries and other baked goods, and a woman had a bright yellow stall with jars of honey stacked on the table.

I looked at all the faces, waiting for the moment one of them changed into a grey-skinned monster, but none did. Tightening my grip on my illusion, I skirted around the edge of the market.

I had no idea where to go. What did people do when they were on the run? They found someplace to hide, but if I wanted the Chimera to follow me and leave the Warren alone, I had to make a commotion.

I wandered down the street, trying to come up with a plan. That's when I caught sight of my reflection in a shop window and winced. I looked as bad as I felt.

My cheek was red and angry, the skin split open,

and the black eye Darby had given to me yesterday was an epic shade of bluish-black.

Raising my hand, I pressed at the cut lightly. It was a reminder of everything that was wrong with me.

Blinking away fresh tears, I turned and walked the other direction. I passed statues, landmarks, museums, and shops. I dodged traffic and crossed roads. I wound through alleys and forgotten paths.

It wasn't long before I found myself at the foot of Arthur's Seat. The extinct volcano rose over Edinburgh, its ragged crags beautiful and wild, its head touching the low-lying clouds.

I decided to cross the road and join the tourists strolling along the path.

Soon it turned into something more closely resembling a trail and I picked my way over the uneven terrain. At the top of the rise, I found the remains of a building—a wall with a crumbling arch, a window, and a door. A faded marker told me it was the remains of Saint Anthony's Chapel. Whoever Saint Anthony was.

With the ruins towering behind me, I sat on a flat rock and watched the city as it faded into the night. In the distance, I saw the lights of the bridges crossing the Firth of Forth estuary. From here, Edinburgh seemed so vast, stretching in all directions around Castle Hill.

As darkness descended around me and the tourists retreated for the warmth of their hotels, I buried my head into my arms and choked back sobs. I was cold, hungry, alone, and everything hurt. *I suck at being a martyr.*

A meow echoed across the hillside and I raised my head with a gasp. A familiar tabby cat prowled out of the darkness, its fur rippling with Colour, and began to brush up against my legs.

"*Ignis*," I scolded, "what are you doing out here, you daft cat? I told you to stay."

Before I could do anything else, a large black German Shepard loped out of the shadows and sat before me. Jaimie lifted his paw and tapped me on the leg, his tongue lolling out the side of this mouth. Looking up, I saw Rory appear out of the fog of his illusion.

"Elspeth, thank *Salle* we found you," he said standing before me.

I glared at Ignis. "*Traitor.*"

"Don't blame the flea bag," Rory stated. "He's only trying to help. Better than a bloodhound, that one." Jaime barked softly in protest. "Well, nearly as good as a German Shepard."

I had nothing to say, so I turned my gaze away.

Rory scuffed his toe against a rock and shoved his hands into his coat pockets. "I'm sorry about what they did to you. It was inexcusable."

I shrugged, the motion sending a throb through the prism burns over my body. I wasn't sure how many there were, but it felt like they were snaked over every part of me.

"Elspeth, I—"

"*Don't.*" I huddled into my scarf, conscious that my face was a complete mess. I must look pathetic. I certainly felt like it sitting before a handsome, powerful Druid and his muscled shapeshifter best friend.

Ignis head-butted my arm, trying to crawl onto my lap, but I gently nudged him away.

"They tried to *murder me*," I muttered. "Your perfect girlfriend led the charge. Vanora—"

"She's not my girlfriend," Rory interrupted.

I ignored him. "Their hatred…" I swallowed the knot in my throat. "There's nothing you or anyone can say to make it go away."

Silence fell over the chapel ruins. I was too ashamed to walk away, so I sat on the rock like a useless lump.

"How did you get out?" Rory finally asked.

"How do you think," I muttered.

He shook his head to cover his confusion. "It's not safe out here. You have to come back."

"I don't have to do anything," I snapped. "You're the one who should have stayed in your magical cave." I glanced at Jaimie. "You too."

"*Elspeth.*"

I rose to my feet and dusted off my arse. "I'm not going back. I can't."

"You can. We need you."

I snorted, scowling at him. "I'm only needed to

ensure the prophecy favours the Druids. That's not the kind of need I subscribe to."

"The portals have been severed," he said. "You won't be able to get back into the Warren without us."

"I don't want to go back," I murmured. "All that's waiting for me there is a slit throat."

Rory stepped towards me. "Then we're coming with you."

"No," my scowl deepened, "don't be stupid. The only thing that follows me is death. The Chimera want me, Rory. If I leave, they'll follow. If you both stay, you'll have a chance at a peaceful life. If you both come with me, they'll kill you to get to me. I've been the catalyst for too much death already."

Jaimie lowered his head and let out a low growl.

"That's dog speak for no way in hell," Rory told me.

"You're not my *neach-gleidhidh* anymore. You're free."

"*Elspeth…*"

I wish my father was here.

That's when inspiration struck—a plan for the perfect commotion began to form in the back of my mind.

I began to walk away, but Rory came after me with Ignis and Jaimie on his heels. I threw my hand up with an exasperated growl and allowed my intent to shape a barrier behind me.

Rory let out a yelp as he smacked into the invisible wall. "Elspeth! *Wait.*"

Don't be such a bitch, Elspeth, I thought. *They're only trying to help.* But so was I. I needed to end this before more Druids died.

I turned. Rory rubbed his nose in bewilderment. He hadn't seen it coming—a testament to my growing ability—but it wasn't quite as comforting as I thought it would be.

"Where will you go?" he asked, looking after me with a mournful expression.

I sighed and turned my back on him. "To make things go back to the way they were."

My internal death sensors led me across the city to Old Calton Cemetery. The irony wasn't lost on me.

It sat in the shadow of Calton Hill, a place that only served to remind me of the day Owen showed his true face. I held my throbbing wrists against my stomach, adrenaline the only thing keeping me on my feet. It'd been one hell of a day.

The gate was secured with a heavy chain and padlock, but I phased through the iron bars and walked up the stairs.

The cemetery itself was a tightly packed pocket of history nestled within the dense inner city. An enormous obelisk dominated the grounds, pointing up to the heavens. The modern streetlights tinted the overcast sky a dull burnt orange, lengthening the shadows into creepy trespasser territory. I shouldn't be here, but no one would notice my passing.

Like Greyfriars, this cemetery had a great deal of above-ground mausoleums, but below ground burials with matching headstones still dotted the lawn in matching numbers. It was beautiful in its grimness—the detail and care put into these final resting places a testament to the love people had for their departed.

My boots crunched against the gravel as I waked up the path, wondering where the best place to contact the dead might be. In the end, I clambered up the side of the wall and onto the lawn. Weaving between headstones, I stood by the lid of a raised stone grave and peered at an ornate mausoleum opposite.

I now knew how things worked. I had no emotional hang-ups blocking me and after everything I'd been through, I believed in the supernatural. I simply had to focus on my intent and imagine it done, then the gift entwined with my blood would do the rest.

Closing my eyes, I pushed away the pain in my body and focused on the one thing I'd wanted since arriving in Scotland.

Then, I stepped into death.

Colour bleached out of the world, the grass turned grey underfoot and the orange sky dulled to black. White fog swirled around the headstones and oozed out of the doors of the mausoleum and curled around my ankles.

I always thought death would be cold, but I didn't feel cold. In fact, I didn't feel *anything*. Death was the absence of life—and life was colour and feeling. Made total sense.

"Els?"

I turned at the sound of my father's voice. He emerged from the fog, tall, strong, and just the way I remembered him. He was grey, gone was his familiar salt and pepper auburn hair, and his brilliant green eyes, the colour of ash.

I choked back a sob and rushed to meet him, but even as I threw myself into his arms, I knew I'd never be able to feel his warmth again.

"Sweetie, what are you doing here?" he murmured, his arms winding around my shaking body. I couldn't feel him, but the gesture was enough for now.

"I needed to see you," I told him, "one last time."

He pulled back, his colourless gaze searching mine. "You know." He looked around, his expression falling as he recognised the shadowy cemetery. "You found them."

"I-I think destiny found me."

"*The prophecy*." It was a hushed whisper, only intended for him, but I heard it.

"This world…" I shook my head, my adventures feeling more like a nightmare. "I can make flowers from magical threads that grow out of my palm," I told him. "Not to mention my useless Arts degree is suddenly viable by combining it with my high school mathematical knowhow. It's an amazing world full of beauty and myth come to life, but…"

Dad raised his hand and traced his fingertips over my cut cheek but his spirit form couldn't connect with mine.

"Finding a connection to what I lost? The cost was too great," I whispered.

After a long moment, he said, "They found me. I was out in the fire zone and I saw an elemental warrior in the blackened forest. I knew I had to kill it before it found you… I… I couldn't stop it. A fire crew was rushing towards me and you—" He choked up, frustrated that he couldn't touch me.

"You sacrificed yourself to save them *and* me. Don't be sorry, Dad."

"Forgive me, Els," he said. "I thought I was protecting you from suffering this life."

"*I know.* I could shout a lot of what ifs at you right now, but none of them matter anymore. So much has happened and I don't have much time. I'm on my own now with a thousand questions, but I…" I thought about Rory, Jaimie, Delilah, and Ignis, knowing I couldn't let them suffer at the hands of the Chimera. I knew what I had to do now—simply leaving wasn't going to be enough. "I have my own crew to save."

"What—"

"*Please listen,*" I interrupted, my depression fading under the promise of the battle I was about to fight. Druids still had the power to open portals and the

Chimera would still break into the Warren, regardless of me being there or not. "The Druids hate me for what I am, and the Chimera want to exploit my power for their own unknown ends. I left the Warren before the Druids could kill me, but the Fae are at their door. They…" I drew in a shaking breath. "I could run and leave them to their fate—I don't think anyone would blame me—but there are good people down there. People who helped me despite my Fae blood."

"Delilah?" Dad asked.

"Grandmother, you mean?"

"Oh, Els. I'm so sorry…" His gaze lowered, and I saw the regret in his tired expression. "I kept so much from you. More than I had a right to. A child should know her mother."

I shook my head, wanting to ask about her so badly but I knew I had no time.

"Dad, if the Chimera get into the Warren and capture the Druids, they will be able to open a portal to their world and people will die. Lots of people. Right now, I have a chance to lure them away. I'm what they want above all else."

"You're offering yourself as bait," he murmured.

"The prophecy is coming true, but I still have a chance to stop it." I curled my lip. "Or buy some time."

"Els—"

The fog shuddered and began to swirl around us. I lifted my head and looked around the cemetery, but

I was too far into the spirit world to see what was going on back in life.

Dad stepped closer, his presence the next best thing to taking my hand. "*The Chimera.*"

"Good," I said. "I was hoping they'd come."

"Elspeth, *you must run.*"

I shook my head. "I know what I need to do now, Dad," I told him. "Don't worry about me."

"Elspeth, you don't understand. The black sun—"

"*Will never rise.*"

I walked back towards life and colour began to bleed into the world once more. I threw one last look over my shoulder at my father and smiled.

"I love you, Dad."

18

The cemetery snapped back into focus and the night sounds of Edinburgh hissed in the background.

I wasn't surprised to see Owen leaning against a headstone. He had a smug expression on his face, like a cat who'd caught a mouse unawares. *Do I have news for you.*

"Couldn't resist talking to daddy?" he asked, a smirk pulling at his lips.

"Nice to see that knife in your heart didn't change your terrible attitude," I drawled.

He snatched my beanie, tearing it off my head. My hair fell free, tumbling around my shoulders.

"Your hair has changed since the last time saw you," he said with a grin. "What a beautiful shade of green."

"Quit it with the arsehole, Owen," I snarled. "I'm

not the same woman you tried to kidnap on top of Calton Hill."

His gaze raked over me. "I can see that. Been in a fight, have you?"

I ignored his baiting. "I think it's time you and I have a frank discussion about what's really going on here."

"They don't know anything about us, do they? You don't even know what kind of Fae you are."

I narrowed my eyes. "If you know what kind of Fae I am, then why not just tell me? Let me make up my own mind instead of letting some indecipherable prophecy decide things. Wouldn't it be better for everyone if I came of my own free will?"

"I meant what I said that day in the close," he told me. "Come with me and I will give you all the answers you deserve."

"Was killing my father necessary?"

"A child shouldn't be without their father, but," Owen sighed, "it had to be done. He stole you from us. Justice had to be served."

I tensed. Everyone thought they were the hero of their own stories. They thought they were doing the right thing, but how much evil was in Owen's heart? The Fae weren't human or Druid—who knew what drove their motivations?

"Tell me something true, Owen. Give me one good reason why I should side with the Chimera, especially after you took the one person I loved the most away from me."

"You want a truth, Elspeth?" He stalked towards me, anger clouding his eyes. "Your mother was supposed to be our queen. That was before your Druid father *stole her from us*. Then he stole you."

"A queen?" That was the last thing I expected him to say.

"And you can take her place, Elspeth."

I made a face. "But I'm half Druid. My father was the man who stole her from your king. Wouldn't that be an insult?" *Just like the reverse is true with the Druids.*

"You carry her blood. You alone, Elspeth. *You can choose.*"

"Choose?"

"Fae or Druid. It's more than just picking a side."

Now I understood why I'd taken so well to my Colours. Through the influence of my father's love, I'd chosen him—and his heritage—without even knowing it. If what Owen was saying was true, then I could allow my Fae blood to dominate. But something in the way he spoke told me it would probably be a mistake.

"What's so special about my mother's blood?" I demanded.

He chuckled. "My, aren't you clever."

"I'm a grown arse woman, Owen," I snapped, "not some weak-willed child ripe for manipulation. Don't you dare patronise me."

"Finally, some fire underneath all that pathetic Druid passiveness."

"Why do you hate the Druids so much? Did my

mother hurt your feelings when she decided to choose love?"

"You have no idea," he snarled. *"I don't care about love.* I've been trapped here for a thousand years. Don't you think I want to go home?" *A thousand years?*

"Is that what this is all about?" I asked. "You want to use my Druid abilities to open a portal to your world so you can bypass the Witches and return me to your king in place of my mother?" It couldn't be that simple. "What will you do once you're there? Who are you fighting?"

"Like I said, come with me and you'll have all the answers you desire." Owen's lip curled into a wicked smile and his illusion flickered. For a split-second, I was treated to his natural form, pointed teeth and all.

Rory said the Chimera were Dark Fae. Evil. What would I be unleashing if I allowed them to reunite their forces? Not to mention the prophecy that involved the Druids. There was so much I didn't understand. Not a good place to be negotiating from.

The only thing I did know was that I wasn't going to be a pawn in a war between the Fae, just as I was in the fight between the Chimera and the Druids.

The more I learned, the more I wondered if it was a case of choosing the lesser evil. Honestly, if that was the case, I'd rather not choose at all.

"And what about the Warren?" I asked. "How many Chimera know of it?"

"Now who's patronising," Owen said with a sneer.

"Not at all," I drawled. "It's a straight-forward

question. It's been twenty-five years and you still haven't captured a Druid. When you finally go home and kneel before your king, he'll probably be looking to put your head on a pike as punishment for your continued failure." I shrugged, keeping up the pretence of nonchalance. "I thought a Fae as clever as you would have a bargaining chip at his disposal. It would be a pity to put in all that work and be rewarded with death."

Owen's eyebrows rose.

"Come now. Isn't this what you want?" I stepped towards him. "My Fae blood is just below the surface, waiting for me to grasp it." I opened my palm and allowed a thread of Druidic Colour to pool. "I don't need much more to turn this into a portal." I smirked and closed my fist around the threads. "The Druids taught me a lot of things, hoping I'd side with them, but as you can see…" I shoved the sleeve of my jacket up, "they weren't as wise as they made themselves out to be."

Owen's gaze fell onto the prism burns and his jaw tensed. He was angry. *Truly angry*. Curious.

"Perhaps I'll find a more welcoming home amongst my mother's people," I continued. "Apparently, I have a king waiting for me."

"Elspeth," he murmured, swallowing my 'confession' hook, line, and sinker, "you have no idea what your return will herald for our people. You will be a *queen*."

I forced a smile onto my lips and took his hands in

mine. "I only need one thing from you, Owen, and I will give you your precious portal."

"*Anything*." His grip tightened around mine and he pulled our joined hands against his chest. "Name it."

"I won't go without proof," I said with a shake of my head. "You've lied to me before. I don't trust that you won't do it again. I need your total and complete honesty."

"Proof?" he asked. "You blood is proof enough. You can go places no one else can."

My blood?

"Oh, Elspeth," he murmured, his cool gaze studying my confused expression. "You have such power. When you learn how to control your family's gift, you will never fear again. You will *control* the hearts of men and Fae alike. I promise you this."

The prophecy came to mind, summoned by Owen's emphasis on the world control. I was a Spirit Walker...*and* the Fae equivalent. I'd phased through the walls of the Warren like they were nothing, just like I'd stepped into the spirit world. I was the master of death and I would call upon the black sun to rise...

I understood now. It was as clear to me as the hate I felt oozing into me through Owen's hands. The Chimera were evil, and the only thing that awaited me in the court of the Dark Fae was terror.

I felt Darkness rise within me, but I wasn't afraid. All I had to do was focus my intent, just like Rory had taught me.

"Don't worry, Owen," I whispered, pressing my

body against his. "I understand perfectly. Thank you for your honesty."

Time slowed and I became essence, swirling around our bodies like a screaming tornado. I saw myself from afar—black eyes bleeding like a devil—and I struck like a snake, venom dripping from my proverbial fangs as I attacked.

My hand curled around Owen's neck and I snarled as the flesh of my hand began to flake and turn black. The flakes floated into the air like charred ash and I phased.

Owen gasped, his eyes widening with fear as my spirit invaded his, twisting and choking the life from him. I was a demon possessing his Chimera soul, and I dragged the truth from him, one scrap at a time.

The images in his mind came to me all at once. A ruined land, a castle carved into a mountain capped with snow, fire and brimstone, black-armoured creatures, a woman with green hair fleeing across a frozen lake, armies clashing on a field of red, an enormous snarled tree rising out of an ancient forest…

It took me a moment to get it all into order, but when I did, the truth was too terrifying to comprehend.

The Chimera wanted to take over the Fae world, then sweep into Earth, destroying the Witches for barring their way home, enslave the Druids, and when they had the power they desired, they would turn on humanity. The Chimera wanted to rule with a dynasty of terror that stretched across multiple worlds. They wanted to become all-powerful.

They wanted to be *gods*.

And my mother? I drove the truth from him, driving into his sprit like a hammer. The woman fleeing across the icy lake was her, but Owen didn't know her face, just the story of her escape.

He was telling the truth about her being destined for the king of the Dark Fae, but it wasn't consensual. They intended to steal her away and turn her to evil, just like they were trying to do to me… *They are trying to turn me to Darkness*. They wanted me to destroy the world—*both of them*.

This was the truth as Owen knew it.

"You figured it out," he rasped, as colour leeched from his body.

"I told you I wasn't the same woman you tried to kidnap on Calton Hill. You should have listened."

I wasn't sure how to feel about the horror I'd found in his mind. All I wanted to do was kill him for his duplicitous lies—and get some kind of revenge for my father. The Warren, and the Druids who huddled inside it, seemed to be so far away.

"Power corrupts, Owen," I drawled. "Your heart is black and your king… He will never have what he desires. I will not enslave innocents on any world."

"At least my heart isn't as black as yours. I can see the sun turning dark already."

"If the black sun rises, it will dawn on the Chimera," I snarled.

Cracks appeared on his cheeks, splintering into ragged shapes that reminded me of the surface of a dry lake.

"And so the wheels of destiny turn," he whispered as his spirit began to crumble. "You have no idea what you've set in motion."

"Too bad you won't be around to see it."

Owen opened his mouth to reply, but it was too little, too late. He fell in on himself, crumbling into a pile of ash. It was a horrific sight, knowing a Fae had once stood there, but how could I feel sympathy for someone whose sole purpose was to twist me into something evil? If anything, all the emotion that beat through my heart was pity.

Dark shadows flitted between the headstones and I raised my head. Owen hadn't come alone.

Chimera emerged from the surrounding cemetery, prowling around me like pack of hungry lions. They hadn't bothered to hide their faces and as they approached, I was treated to their full grey-skinned, pointy teeth, gremlin glory.

I was in big trouble, but I had one saving grace— the pile of ash at my feet.

The millions dollar question was, could I do it again? I guess I was about to find out.

"Okay, guys," I said, sounding much more confident than I felt, "I guess we're doing this."

19

"Any last words?" I asked, counting the Chimera circling through the cemetery.

Six.

One of the Fae stepped towards me, his sword glinting in the glow of the orange street light.

"You killed our master," he said. His pointed teeth gave him a lisp, reminding me of a certain hissing reptile.

"You king will be pissed if you kill me," I said.

"Our king is not here."

A roar bellowed from behind me and a blur leapt over my shoulder and collided with the Chimera. The sword flew from his grasp, clattering against the side of a crumbling mausoleum.

A tiger with glowing blue stripes mauled the Fae, swatting him with huge clawed paws.

Ignis. I'd know that daft cat anywhere.

Nothing in this world surprised me anymore.

The Chimera screamed as the tiger clamped its jaws around his neck. A snap echoed through the cemetery and the Fae were still.

Five pairs of eyes glared at me out of the gloom and the glint of metal told me that they didn't come unarmed. Ignis prowled towards me, putting himself between me and the enemy.

The challenge was clear, but I had nothing to fight with—no knife, no sword, no skills—just a dangerous power I didn't know the limits of.

Get a grip, Elspeth. Now wasn't the time to fear what I might become. I had to grab hold of my destiny and make it my own…or die trying.

"Ignis? I appreciate the assist, but give me some room, will you?"

The tiger purred, licked his whiskers, and prowled through the shadows. His blue glow ebbed in the dark, letting me know where he was.

Focusing on the remaining Chimera, I hoped this worked.

I let go of the final barrier between me and the Fae blood swirling through my veins…and became black essence.

The cemetery went dark, all the light from the city blinking out, and the shadows began to rise. I took one step forwards and a black vicious liquid rose in my wake, floating in the sky as if gravity ceased to exist.

The Chimera hesitated, their eyes widening in fear.

They want to kill you, a voice echoed in my head. *They want to cut you open and tear your insides out.*

I looked to a shadow at my side. *Mother?*

It hissed and dove at me, slamming into my body and feeding the power that rose within me.

Kill them, kill them, kill them. They are the enemy.

My head snapped to the front.

Let me go. Let me go now!

I raised my hands, balking at the bluish hue my skin had taken. My gaze focused through a filmy haze of shadow and the Darkness rose up from the ground and encircled the Chimera.

The essence was me, yet it was something else. Something wild and elemental…beyond this reality.

The oozing black liquid crawled over the Fae, consuming them one by one—strangling, suffocating. I drew them into death, Colour binding them, and five souls became shadow then drifted away into the currents of death like sand blown in the wind.

Power rose behind me and I swung around, but I was too late to stop the unseen sword arcing towards my neck. Closing my eyes, I felt the Darkness seethe.

The sharp sound of metal colliding with metal rang through the air. My eyes jerked open and I gasped when I saw Rory locked in a tight grapple with the Chimera.

Their swords rasped as they slid together, then they broke apart and the Druid spun, the blade hissing through the air…and cut the Fae's head clean off its shoulders.

Jaimie appeared behind him, his German Shepard form padding between the headstones.

My head snapped up and I stared at them through the film of darkness. *More?*

"Get out of here," I rasped. *"I can't hold it."*

Rory dropped the sword and threw his arms around my trembling body. His Colours flared as he held onto me and the Darkness began to subside. I didn't know if it was conscious or if it sensed his intent, but whatever I'd unleashed seemed to have run its course.

I slammed my Colour around the Dark things and began to shake. If it wasn't for Rory, I would have fallen to my knees.

"Are you all right?" he asked, drawing back. He smoothed my hair behind my ears.

"I-I don't know."

His thumb brushed over my cheek. "The cut it gone. So is your black eye."

I raised my hand to my face and found he was right. The prism burns didn't seem to sting anymore, either. "My eyes?"

"Green as two shiny emeralds."

I sighed. I was Elspeth again.

"It felt like that day in the close," I said. "Like it was going to explode."

"Whatever *it* was, it knew we were your friends," Rory told me.

Now in his human form, Jaimie stood to the side.

One hand covered his junk and the other swatted at Rory. "Help a man out, will you?"

Rory chuckled, shucked off his coat, and tossed it to the Druid.

Ignis leapt onto the headstone beside me and meowed, pawing the air. He was a tabby cat again, but no less needy.

Rory scratched him on the head. "Your cat is really something, huh? He must have had some serious magic of his own when he was alive."

Nervousness crept into my heart and I glanced between the Druids.

"How long were you…" I edged backwards.

"Uh, a while," Jaimie admitted.

They'd seen me talking with Owen, then. They'd likely heard our conversation…and seen me turn him into a pile of ash.

"You thought I was going with him, didn't you?" I asked.

Rory shook his head. "*Never.*"

I glanced at Jaimie. "I just wanted answers."

"I know, lass," the shapeshifter said. "They were hard won…and we didn't help when we should've."

"You were there when it counted," I told him, glancing at the dead Chimera. "That's all that matters."

I was the black sun.

The revelation hit me like a tonne of bricks. *When the black sun rises, death will choose the hand of fate.* My power would choose who lived and died, not me—not unless I learned how to control it.

"The Warren should be safe now," I said. "I forced the truth from Owen. Well, the truth as he knew it."

"What does that mean?" Jaimie asked.

"It means time will tell if the knowledge spread without his knowing."

And everything he told me about the Fae and my mother might be a lie fed to him to keep him obedient. There was nothing better at keeping trapped fanatical soldiers loyal than blind faith.

"Elspeth?"

I must have been silent for a long time. I blinked and knew what I had to do. I'd been doing it all my life, so it wouldn't be much of a stretch.

I stood before Rory. "Do you understand what I am?"

"You're not ascending, are you?" he murmured.

I shook my head. "No, I'm not."

"It's astral projection," Jaimie said. "You projected your soul, lass."

"That's a kind way of putting it, I suppose."

"You projected your soul inside the Chimera?" Rory asked, his brow furrowing.

"I possessed him, Rory. I controlled him, took his truth, and broke everything he was." I shook my head. "You know Delilah's shattered souls? What I did to Owen was *worse…and it was easy.*" I swept my arm around, gesturing to the fallen Chimera. "And then I pulled his friends into death and turned them inside out. Cutting off that guy's head was kinder." The Druids stared at me in shock. They didn't understand, but neither did I. "Whatever kind of Fae I truly am, I can't say for sure, but mixed with my ability to Spirit Walk… All I have to do is will it and I could enslave you all by accident. I can't go back."

"Of course, you can come back," Rory said. "The Warren is your home."

"You don't understand. I had no control. *None*. Once the Darkness took hold, I had to let it run its course. If I did that in the Warren?" I shook my head and sighed. "They were right to try to kill me."

"No," he snarled, grabbing my arm. "Don't say that, Elspeth. Let me help you control it. I—"

"She's right, Rory," Jaimie said, placing a big hand on the Druid's shoulder. "I don't like it either, but her power is unstable. Until she can handle it, going back to the Warren isn't the best idea."

"But you can't go alone," Rory argued.

"This power…it makes me Dark, Rory. I can feel it. It's like…" I pressed my fist against my heart. "It's like someone else is living inside me and I just let them out of their cage."

"Your power is not who you are, Elspeth," he murmured. "You have a good heart. You're kind, funny, sweet, caring—"

"Maybe," I said, "but it isn't enough. I need to go, and it has to be on my own. This won't be the last we see of the Chimera and they have to follow me if the

Warren is to remain hidden." I felt Ignis' paw tap on my shoulder and I looked up at the cat. "Stay with the Druids…and please listen this time."

Picking up my beanie, I dusted the dirt off and put it back on my head.

Rory was watching me with a forlorn expression that tugged at my heartstrings. He truly cared about me. I'd wanted someone to look at me like that my entire life, but now that someone was, I had to turn them away. The world was a cruel place for people like me—people wrapped up in a prophecy of extinction.

"Don't worry," I told them, "I'll figure it out."

"I know you probably won't need it, but…" Rory pulled the knife and matching scabbard from his belt and handed them to me, "best not go unprepared."

"Are you sure?"

"Where will you go?" Rory asked, pressing the knife towards me.

I shrugged. "Who knows? I have a cool teleporting power. Maybe I'll go to the Bahamas."

"Lass," Jaimie stepped forwards and put his hands on my shoulders, "if you ever need help, all you need to do is call."

"Thank you." I glanced at Rory. "For *everything*."

20

______

W|averley Station was buzzing.

The early morning rush hour was well underway. Overhead, automated announcements blared out of speakers. *The next train to depart from platform four, is the eight-forty-five ScotRail service to Glasgow Central, stopping at Haymarket, Linlithgow…*

Ticket barriers squealed as they opened and banged as they shut. People lingered at the departure displays, waiting for their trains to be announced while others circled the *WH Smith* looking at magazines and purchasing sweets.

I nursed a can of energy drink between my knees and looked up at the display and checked my ticket. The 9:08 Virgin Trains service to London Euston was twenty-four minutes away and the platform wasn't ready yet. It was less than half an hour, but the time was dragging after the night I'd had.

I sighed at the cost, which was quite a blow to my

wallet, but I didn't think I'd get away with fare evading with my Druid illusion in a tightly packed train carriage. I was on the run now, and that meant I had to be careful.

The Chimera were ingrained in the police and most likely other government institutions, so if I used my credit card, they'd be on me like moths to a flame. A cashless society wasn't for me.

Besides, the Darkness was back in its box and I wasn't going to let it out any time soon. For now, I was just a plain Druid with meagre fighting skills.

I watched the humans do as their namesake and sighed. Everyone had someplace to be, and I felt like the only person in the world who didn't know where she was going.

Someone sat next to me and I looked up at Delilah.

"You can't change my mind," I told her.

"Humour an old woman."

"You don't look a day over fifty."

"Fifty?" She raised a hand and prodded at the fine wrinkles around her eyes. "I'm losing my touch."

We sat and watched people walk across the overpass above the concourse for a few minutes. There wasn't a Fae amongst them.

"The Warren is safe," Delilah said. "The Chimera who knew of its existence have perished."

"It's still not safe. Not while I'm around."

"The Druids know what you did for them.

Raurich and Jaimie made sure of it. You will be welcomed back, granddaughter."

"Perhaps, but there will always be an underlying prejudice towards me," I said. "I'll never belong. Not really. My dad hid me because I'm half Fae. He knew I wouldn't be accepted." But even he didn't know what I'd be capable of.

"No, I think it's more than that," Delilah mused. "You are a curious woman, Elspeth Quarrie, Spirit Walker."

"*Dead in darkness*," I whispered. "*When the black sun rises, death will choose the hand of fate.*" The clues were there all along.

"Prophecies rarely manifest as they are spoken," she told me. "The black sun could mean any number of things. Worrying will not achieve anything, Elspeth. Follow your conscious."

"My conscious is telling me to leave before I cause more harm."

The Druidess sighed. "Fair enough. I see you cannot be swayed."

"You're an Elder, surely you can understand why I'm doing this?"

"In this moment, I'm your grandmother, Elspeth. My heart doesn't want to let you go, but I know I must let you create your own destiny. If anyone can change fate, it's you."

I shook my head. "How do you know?"

She smiled softly. "Call it a hunch."

I snorted and shook my head. I wanted to believe

her, but I had so much to figure out before I could form my own opinion on the matter.

"I have a gift for you." She reached into her bag and pulled out a book.

It was one of those fancy journals with a wraparound cover that fastened with a matching strip of leather. This one was about an A6 in size and a deep chocolate colour. Dents and scratches marred the leather—it had seen a great deal of use—and vibrated with a curious echo of Colour.

Offering it to me, she added, "It's your father's journal. His portal research."

Eyeing the journal with suspicion, I asked, "Why would you give this to me?"

"Perhaps it holds a clue only his daughter would understand…or perhaps it's simply because his daughter has the only right to possess it."

I took it and stared at the cover. I wanted to open it right there and then, but whatever was inside felt like it should be read without the eyes of Delilah and all of Edinburgh looking on.

"And what's this?" Eyeing Rory's knife poking out from underneath my jacket, she clucked her tongue in disapproval. "You should carry that where no one will see it."

"I have an illusion on it."

Delilah huffed and unslung the strap of her bag. Taking out her purse, she handed the embroidered black bag to me. "Here. A parting gift."

"Oh, I couldn't."

"You need something to carry that knife in."

I held the bag in my lap and studied the outside. One side was covered with a blue, purple, and grey mandala—or a Druidic prism to the trained eye. The design was embellished with gaudy plastic jewels and tiny seed beads—totally Delilah's style.

I slipped the knife inside, along with my coin purse and passport, noticing there was an internal compartment, along with a bar of chocolate, an unopened packet of tissues, and a little travel-sized bottle of hand sanitiser. She was an Elder but still a grandmother at heart.

"Thanks," I said, zipping the bag closed.

The platform number appeared on the departures board and I rose.

Delilah stood. "Safe journey, Elspeth."

I looked at her and decided we were close enough now to give her a hug. We embraced for a moment before I drew back.

"Goodbye," I murmured. "Look after Ignis for me?"

She smiled. "Of course."

I took the stairs up to the overpass two at a time, resisting the urge to look back. It wouldn't matter anyway. Delilah would already be gone, her illusion covering all traces of her ever being here.

I descended to the platform, clutching my new bag close, feeling the weight of my father's journal as it hit a steady beat against my leg. The train was waiting and people were climbing aboard.

I have the power to help, he'd told me. *And when the Earth and her creatures cry out in pain, we should answer with our whole hearts.*

Checking my ticket, I found carriage B and lingered outside the automatic door. Edinburgh was cold this morning and a misty drizzle fluttered against my flushed cheeks. It really was a beautiful city.

The platform attendant blew their whistle, signalling the train was about to depart. I looked at the door, then at my father's journal.

"Miss?" the attendant called out, waving his hand to get my attention. "Are you getting on?"

I looked back at the city, spotting the very tip of Castle Hill rising above the buildings bordering the station.

"*Miss?* The train is about to depart."

"*Bò bhrònach.*" I turned my face towards the sky and began to laugh as I realised what it meant. "Stupid cow."

Did Elspeth get on the train? Will Ignis really listen this time and stay with the Druids?
Find out in **ARCANE SPIRIT**, *the second novel in The Darkland Druids series.*

OTHER BOOKS IN THE DARKLAND DRUIDS

by Nicole R. Taylor

Druids, **Witches**, **Fae**, and **shapeshifters** abound in this thrilling magical adventure!

Arcane Rising #1
Arcane Spirit #2
Arcane Mythos #3
Arcane Revenant #4

ABOUT NICOLE

Nicole R. Taylor is an Australian Urban Fantasy author.

She lives in the western suburbs of Melbourne dreaming up nail biting stories featuring sassy witches, duplicitous vampires, hunky shapeshifters, and devious monsters.

She likes chocolate, cat memes, and video games.

When she's not writing, she likes to think of what she's writing next.

Follow Nicole Online:

Website: www.nicolertaylorwrites.com
Facebook: facebook.com/nrtaylorwrites
Newsletter: www.nicolertaylorwrites.com/newsletter
Email: nicole.this.is@gmail.com

ARCANE SPIRIT
(THE DARKLAND DRUIDS - BOOK TWO)

A prophecy of doom. A destiny she cannot escape. When the black sun rises, death will choose the hand of fate.

The real **Elspeth Quarrie** has awoken, and with her comes a prophecy of extinction.

Her dark Fae power, known as the black sun, will destroy everyone she's come to care about…unless she can rewrite a destiny given to her before she was even born.

But thwarting the threads of fate was never going to be that easy.

Now her spirit has awoken, Elspeth finds herself hunted by the ruthless Chimera — the dark sect of Fae warriors who are desperate to use her powers for evil. She knows its only a matter of time before she's forced to fight. . . and when she does, she risks triggering the prophecy and destroying everyone she cares about.

Elspeth is determined to master her abilities before the Chimera find her. . . but is it already too late?

To find out, Elspeth will have to go to war.

Or risk the black sun rising.

***Arcane Spirit** is the second book of **The Darkland Druids**, a mystical Urban Fantasy series set in modern day Scotland.*

A lost woman tied to a prophecy of death may be the Druids only chance at finally finding peace in Scotland. . . or the key to giving the forces of evil the power they need to rule over everything. Druids and Fae go head to head in this gripping fantasy saga!

Want more novels just like this one? Check out Nicole's other series:

THE ARONDIGHT CODEX - An ancient war with demons. A lost sword with the power to end it all. And a woman with purple hair is the world's only hope.

THE CAMELOT ARCHIVE - Set in the same alternate Arthurian world seen in **The Arondight Codex**… Deadly secrets. Murder and revenge. The end of the world is nye and Camelot is the last bastion of hope.

THE WITCH HUNTER SAGA - Vampires and witches collide in this thrilling Urban Fantasy adventure. You've never met vampires quite like these…

THE CRESCENT WITCH CHRONICLES - Witches, shapeshifters, and ancient myth collide in this colourful Irish flavoured series! Come on an adventure fraught with danger and forbidden romance… and the ultimate battle to save magic before it's gone forever.

THE DARKLAND DRUIDS - A woman with no living relatives travels from Australia to the other side of the world to find out the truth of who she is…only to land in the middle of a prophecy of destruction. Druids, witches, fae, and shapeshifters abound in this thrilling magical adventure!

Find out more at: NicoleRTaylorWrites.com

See what titles are FREE at: Nicole's Free Reads

www.ingramcontent.com/pod-product-compliance
Lightning Source LLC
Chambersburg PA
CBHW030748190728
48285CB00003B/728